Fire!

"What's going on?" Christina cried, squinting in the bright light.

"Someone's yelling 'fire.'" Grabbing a shirt, Melanie slipped it on over her nightie. She was the first out the door.

Several other campers had woken up and were milling around outside. Melanie ran swiftly across the lawn, in bare feet, slowing between the carriage house and the big house. There was no sign of fire in either of the buildings.

The barns! Spinning, she looked down the hill. Her heart leaped into her throat.

Smoke and flames billowed from the storage shed. It was filled with hay and sawdust. Melanie knew that any second, it might burst into flames.

She raced down the hill. Trib, Sterling, Flash, and Geronimo were in the stalls closest to the shed. She had to get them out of the barn before it caught on fire, too!

Don't miss these exciting books from HarperPaperbacks!

Collect all the books in the THOROUGHBRED series:

THOROUGHBRED Super Editions:

*coming soon

ATTENTION: ORGANIZATIONS AND CORPORATIONS

Most HarperPaperbacks are available at special quantity discounts for bulk purchases for sales promotions, premiums, or fund-raising. For information, please call or write:
Special Markets Department, HarperCollins Publishers, 10 East 53rd Street, New York, NY 10022-5299.
Telephone: (212) 207-7528. Fax: (212) 207-7222.

THOROUGHBRED

MELANIE'S LAST RIDE

CREATED BY
JOANNA CAMPBELL

WRITTEN BY
ALICE LEONHARDT

HarperPaperbacks
A Division of HarperCollinsPublishers

▲ HarperPaperbacks
A Division of HarperCollins*Publishers*
10 East 53rd Street, New York, NY 10022-5299

This is a work of fiction. The characters, incidents, and
dialogues are products of the author's imagination and are not to
be construed as real. Any resemblance to actual events or
persons, living or dead, is entirely coincidental.

ISBN 0-06-106531-5

HarperCollins®, ▲ ®, and HarperPaperbacks™
are trademarks of HarperCollins Publishers, Inc.

Cover art © 1998 by Daniel Weiss Associates, Inc.

First printing: August 1998

Printed in the United States of America

Visit HarperPaperbacks on the World Wide Web at
http://www.harpercollins.com

❖ 10 9 8 7 6 5 4 3 2 1

1

"AT LEAST YOU STILL LOVE ME, DON'T YOU, TRIB?" TWELVE-year-old Melanie Graham said to her pony, Tribulation. Not that Trib was really *her* pony, Melanie reminded herself. She was just borrowing him from her cousin, Christina Reese.

Trib turned his head to look at her, a hunk of hay dangling from his mouth. Melanie ruffled his fuzzy mane, then finished currying a manure stain on his flank. Her morning riding lesson was in thirty minutes, and Trib had to look perfect for inspection.

With a sudden sigh, Melanie leaned back against the stall wall. Outside, she heard the happy chatter of the other campers assigned to A barn. This was the beginning of the second week of Camp Saddlebrook's event clinic. Melanie had had a terrific time riding and making new friends. But yesterday when her father hadn't shown up for the Parents' Day activities, she'd been so disappointed. A familiar sadness had crept over her.

It still lingered this morning.

Oh, just forget about him, Melanie told herself as she went back to rubbing Trib vigorously. Too vigorously, Trib told her with a swat of his tail.

"Sorry, Trib," Melanie apologized. "I'm just angry at my dad."

Not that she wasn't used to being stood up. Her father, Will Graham, was a record producer in New York. He'd become so successful—flying from coast to coast almost every week—that he had little time for his daughter. That was one reason Melanie had gone to live with her aunt and uncle, Ashleigh Griffen and Michael Reese, on their horse farm in Kentucky for the summer.

"Hey!" Christina Reese stuck her head into Trib's stall. Her long strawberry-blond hair was windblown, her freckled nose sunburned. "We need you out here before Eliza comes down from the big house."

"What for?" Melanie asked but Christina had already gone. Walking over to the door, Melanie peered around the jamb. The aisle of A barn was filled with campers.

"Jennifer, what's going on?" Melanie called. Jennifer's horse, Geronimo, was also in A barn. Fourteen-year-old Jennifer was on the same team as Eliza, Christina, and Melanie.

Jennifer hurried over, her dark eyes sparkling with excitement.

2

"We made a big sign that says 'congratulations' and put a ribbon on Flash's new halter," Jennifer told her. "Eliza's still inside the house talking to Perky about buying Flash, but she should be here any minute."

"That's so cool!" Melanie's sadness lifted as she thought how happy Eliza had been this morning. Flash, the big Thoroughbred Eliza had borrowed from her instructor for the clinic, had almost been sold to someone else. But thanks to yesterday's rock concert that Melanie's dad arranged, the campers had raised enough money for Eliza to buy the horse through the Young Riders program.

Dropping her curry comb in her grooming bucket, Melanie went to join the others. Sean Laslow and Dylan Becker, the only two male campers, hung back from the rest of the group. As Melanie approached, she noticed Sean's hands were jammed in the pockets of his riding breeches and a sullen expression clouded his cute face.

"What's wrong with you? Is Dylan's snoring keeping you up at night?" Melanie teased.

"Hey, he's the one who talks in his sleep," Dylan shot back, his grin playful. The two boys shared a room above the old carriage house while the girls slept in the dorm-like rooms called the kennels, where the farm's foxhounds had once been housed.

"Dylan!" someone called. Rachel Greenberg was hurrying across the green that separated A barn from B barn. Her long black hair, pulled back in a ponytail, bounced as she ran; her riding helmet was propped under her arm.

By now, everybody at camp knew that Christina and Dylan liked each other. Everybody, that is, except Rachel, who seemed determined to make Dylan interested in her.

"Good morning, Rachel," Melanie said with exaggerated sweetness. Ignoring her, Rachel walked right up to Dylan. Dylan greeted her with a big smile. *Too bad Dylan was such a nice guy*, Melanie thought. *He'd never tell Rachel to get lost.*

Melanie turned her attention back to Sean, who was slouched against a support pillar. Melanie knew he'd been disappointed yesterday, too. He and his teammates—Rachel, Dylan, and Bekka Jenson—had come in last in the quadrille competition. Sean had taken the loss hard, especially when his parents had chastised him in front of everybody at the picnic after the performances.

Still, at least his parents had been there, Melanie thought. Her father hadn't even bothered to call to tell her he couldn't make it until the last minute.

"You okay?" she asked Sean.

"Why shouldn't I be?" he said gruffly, and Melanie knew that he *wasn't* okay. All last week Sean had been the camp's clown and joke-teller. This morning, he seemed like a different kid.

"I just knew you were disappointed in the quadrille yesterday," Melanie continued.

4

He shrugged. "Nah. The quadrille was just some stupid exercise Perky thought up to torture us with."

I thought it was fun, Melanie was about to say, but she quickly swallowed her words. Sean didn't look like he was in the mood to hear them.

"She's coming!" Jennifer called in a low voice. Melanie looked toward the house. Christina was walking down the hill with Eliza. She was gesturing dramatically as if trying to keep Eliza's attention on her.

When the two got about fifty yards away from the barn, Jennifer led a chorus of "congratulations!" Eliza's eyes widened in surprise, and she pressed her hand to her mouth as if to keep from crying.

Melanie knew how the older girl felt. Right now, she didn't have a horse of her own either. Back at Whitebrook Farm, she rode Pirate, a blind ex-racehorse. But that was to help pony the young Thoroughbreds to and from the training track. For lessons, she was riding Trib, Chris-tina's outgrown pony. She and the rambunctious Trib got along great, but it wasn't like having your own horse to love.

Some day I'll have one, Melanie thought. *When I'm back home.* She loved staying at Whitebrook, but it wasn't home. Being away at camp had reminded her of that. Not that she was homesick for New York City. But she missed her dad . . . lots.

"Three cheers for Christina!" someone hollered.

Melanie watched her cousin's face turn bright red with embarrassment. When Christina had found out

5

about the possibility of Eliza losing Flash, she'd come up with the idea for "Operation Flash." After that, all the campers had pitched in to help organize the concert and raise money.

"How about three cheers for Melanie!" Christina chimed in, and the next thing Melanie knew, she was being propelled toward Eliza and her cousin.

"What—?" Melanie sputtered as she stumbled into Eliza.

Eliza gave her an awkward hug. "Thanks to you, too, Mel. If your dad hadn't arranged for Harvey and the Headknockers to play, we never would have earned enough money. They were awesome."

"It was nothing." Melanie gave a mock bow. "You just need the right connections."

"I'll have to call your father and thank him," Eliza added.

"Yeah and remind him he has a daughter," Melanie muttered under her breath.

Christina nudged her with her elbow. "Lighten up," she whispered. "This is Eliza's big moment."

"Tah da!" several voices chorused.

Melanie turned toward the barn. Jennifer was leading Flash from his stall. The handsome black Thoroughbred took one step into the sunlight and halted in his tracks. Nostrils flared, head high, he stared at the crowd of kids.

"Silly goose," Eliza said as she took the lead from Jennifer. "They're not here to buy you. You're mine now." She flung her arms around his neck, suddenly noticing the new leather halter with its brass nameplate on the cheekpiece. "What's this?"

"We didn't have time to get Flash's name engraved on it," Melanie apologized. What she didn't say was that when she and Christina had bought it on Saturday before the concert, they were afraid to get a name etched on it in case Operation Flash was a dismal failure.

"You guys are so cool!" Eliza exclaimed, tears filling her green eyes. "I can't believe it."

"I can't believe it, either!" a harsh voice cut in.

Melanie swung around. Dana Edwards, one of the junior instructors, stood right behind her. Hands on her hips, she was scowling at the campers. Dana was sixteen, with sunlight-streaked, shoulder-length hair. Melanie thought she would have been pretty if she didn't always have such a sour look on her face.

"You all have a lesson in ten minutes," Dana said as campers scurried off in all directions. "And nobody's ready. If you're not in the ring on time, you'll lose points." Dana was in charge of A barn. Bossy, with a big chip on her shoulder, she loved to dock points for any little infraction.

"Aye, aye, captain!" Melanie saluted crisply. Turning sharply on her boot heels, she marched with exaggerated steps to Trib's stall. She could feel Dana right behind her.

Melanie knew she'd ticked her off but she didn't

care. Dana and her list of stupid rules were getting annoying.

"Pitchfork propped against the wall. Top door unlatched. Tack trunk left open." Dana counted off on her fingers. "Those aren't warnings, either, Melanie. Wave your points good-bye."

Giving Melanie a haughty look, Dana headed down the aisle to check the other stall areas. Melanie stuck her tongue out at her. She knew the camp had to have rules, but Dana went overboard.

Outside Sterling's stall, Christina was sweeping the aisle, her back to Dana. As Dana approached, Christina whisked a cloud of dirt and hay in her direction.

Fanning the air, Dana coughed and gagged. "Christina!"

Christina jumped. "Oh, I'm so sorry!"

Clapping a hand over her mouth, Melanie held in a giggle. Served Dana right.

She opened Trib's door and grabbed the brush from the grooming box. After dipping the bristles in his water bucket, she once again tackled the manure stain on his flank. Trib had a white patch on his hind leg, and for some reason he always slept in a pile of manure. If she didn't get it clean, Dana would take off even more points.

Melanie hated the point system. At the beginning of the day, each camper started with eight points. As the day went on, the junior instructors inspected the stalls, barn area, tack, and trunk, and subtracted points for anything they found wrong. And Dana found plenty wrong.

A nip on her backside made Melanie spin around. Ears pricked, Trib stared impishly at her. "Hey, brat, you don't have to bite me to get my attention," she scolded, but her voice was affectionate.

"But you're right, we better hurry," she added as she went into the aisle and pulled her bridle from the tack trunk. "We have only ten minutes to get out to the ring. So don't clamp your teeth when I try and put the bit in your mouth, okay?"

She held up the bridle. Trib took one look at it and ducked into the corner of the stall, his rear toward her. Melanie blew out her breath. Trib was as ornery as he was cute, and she was always having to figure out new tricks to get him to cooperate.

Bribery, she decided. Rummaging through her trunk, she found a granola bar. As she unwrapped it, crumbs rained to the bottom of the trunk.

"You just lost two more points," she said under her breath, mimicking Dana.

Jennifer came down the aisle, leading Geronimo. "Aren't you tacked up yet?"

Melanie straightened. "No. I had to clean off Trib's—"

"Mel!" Christina came up beside Jennifer. Sterling Dream, Christina's Thoroughbred, was saddled and bridled. Melanie noticed the mare's dappled-gray coat shone in the sunlight. Why didn't anyone else's horse roll in manure? "You're going to make us lose points!"

9

"I know!" Melanie retorted. "You guys don't have to remind me. Go on to the ring. I'll be there in a minute."

"We're in the dressage arena," Jennifer corrected. "Didn't you listen at breakfast?"

"And hurry!" Christina said as she followed Jennifer and Geronimo.

Melanie watched them go, a sour feeling filling her stomach. She knew she should care about the points. After Sunday's quadrille demonstration, her team was in second place. That meant every point counted if they were going to win the team trophy at the end of camp.

Turning, Melanie went into the stall with the bridle. Trib shot her a crabby look. Melanie held out the granola bar and his eyes brightened. While he was happily munching, she quickly slipped the bridle on, then saddled him.

For the past week, Melanie had been gung ho about lessons and winning points, too. She wanted to prove to her dad what a good, responsible rider she had become. She wanted to show him that living with Christina and her family had been good for her. Then he'd let her stay at Whitebrook—at least for the rest of the summer. But when he hadn't shown up for Parents' Day, her excitement had died.

In two weeks, at the end of camp, Saddlebrook was having their final event. Saturday all the campers would compete in dressage and cross-country. Sunday would be show jumping and the awards. Like all the campers, Melanie had been really looking forward to it.

She suddenly realized as she threw the stall door open and led Trib out that she didn't care. *Why bother getting excited,* she decided gloomily. Her dad probably wouldn't show up for the final competition, either.

2

STOPPING TRIB BY HER TACK TRUNK, MELANIE PULLED OUT
her riding helmet and plunked it on her head. As she
snapped the chin strap, she glanced around. Except for
a few chirping sparrows, the barn was deserted.

She must be really late.

"Come on, Trib." Clucking to the pony, she started
down the aisle at a jog. But Trib was in no hurry and no
matter how hard she tugged on the reins, he would
only walk across the green and up the hill toward the
dressage arena.

The other riders in the morning's lesson group were
mounted and waiting in the warm-up area. Melanie
spotted Jennifer and Geronimo and Christina and
Sterling who were on her team. Anita and her buckskin
pony, Mushroom; Poe and her chubby bay horse, Pork
Chop; and Rachel and her Arabian mare, Nymph, were
from the other teams.

Frieda Bruder, one of the directors of the camp, was standing in the middle of the cluster of horses. She wore baggy shorts, a sleeveless shirt, and a straw hat. She had such a booming voice that Melanie could hear her a hundred yards away.

By the time Melanie reached the warm-up area, the other riders were in the large field.

"You are late!" Ms. Bruder declared in a German accent.

Melanie only nodded. She didn't think the woman expected an answer.

Hurrying, she looped the reins over Trib's head, then stuck her boot toe in the stirrup to mount. When she started to swing up, the saddle slipped sideways. Losing her balance, she hopped on one leg, then fell backward. Before Melanie hit the ground, Ms. Bruder caught her with strong arms and propelled her to her feet.

"You did not check your girth?" Ms. Bruder sounded as appalled as if Melanie had forgotten to wear pants.

Oops. Melanie's cheeks turned crimson. She knew you were supposed to check your girth before you mounted, especially if you were riding a devious pony who puffed out his belly when you first saddled him.

"I, um, forgot," she stammered.

Ms. Bruder harrumphed as she readjusted the saddle on Trib's chubby withers. Lifting up the flap, she took hold of the girth straps and tugged hard.

Trib gave a grunt, and when Melanie carefully rechecked the girth before mounting, it was tight as a rubber band.

"Thank you," Melanie said, but Ms. Bruder was striding to the middle of the warm-up field yelling, "Backs straight! Elbows relaxed!"

As Melanie steered Trib into the group, Anita rode past. When she glanced in Melanie's direction, she pressed her lips together as if she was trying to hold back an explosion of laughter.

Oh, great. Melanie rolled her eyes. Everyone must have seen her fall. With her luck, Dana was probably hiding behind a tree, subtracting points.

"Working trot!" Ms. Bruder called, rolling the "tr" with her tongue.

Trib picked up a lively trot. Christina and Sterling were just ahead. Whinnying to his barn buddy, Trib hurried to catch up with Sterling. Melanie was posting so fast, she felt as if she was going to bounce right out of the saddle.

"Easy, Trib." She tried to do a half-halt to slow his pace. Jody, one of the senior instructors, had explained that a half-halt was more effective than tugging on the reins. But Melanie could never figure out how to sit in the saddle when Trib's bouncy gait was throwing her in the opposite direction.

"Young lady!" Ms. Bruder hollered. Melanie looked around, realizing the "young lady" meant her. "Turn that pony in a circle until he slows down."

Melanie tightened the inside rein. Trib bent his body to the right, but kept plowing forward.

"Circle him! Put your inside leg on the girth, your outside leg behind and make your pony—"

"Yellow jackets!"

The cry cut off the rest of Ms. Bruder's words.

Melanie snapped her chin up. In front of her, Anita was twisted in her saddle, pointing at the ground. Melanie could see small black-and-yellow-striped insects rising in the air. "Whoa!" she screamed to Trib, but it was too late. He trotted right over the nest. Melanie screeched as a yellow jacket darted at her face.

She could hear Trib's tail whipping in the air, and he began to crowhop. Then he ducked his head and bucked furiously.

Melanie flew over his neck. Tumbling to the ground, she landed on her bottom. Instantly, something sharp whacked her cheek, then her neck.

Shutting her eyes, Melanie swatted blindly. She knew she should get up and run, but she was so freaked by the dive-bombing insects, she couldn't stop flailing her arms.

Suddenly, someone grabbed her wrist and jerked her to her feet. Then the person scooped her up and took off across the field as if Melanie didn't weigh a thing.

As Melanie jounced in the person's arms, she looked up, glimpsing Ms. Bruder's chin. The woman's neck was bright red, and as she ran, she puffed with each step.

"There!" Ms. Bruder ducked behind a tree and

Melanie slid from her arms. Holding her hand over her heart, the instructor gasped for air. Her hat had flown off and trickles of sweat ran down her temples.

"Are you all right?" Melanie asked.

She nodded. "Did we outrun them?" Ms. Bruder asked when she finally caught her breath.

Melanie peered around the tree trunk. The field was empty. Christina, Jennifer, Poe, Rachel, Anita, and their horses had retreated to the other side of the dressage arena. Trib was nowhere in sight. Melanie figured he had high-tailed it back to his stall.

"I think so," Melanie said. "But I don't want to be the one to find out." She touched her cheek and neck. Already, they felt hot, sore and swollen. "Thank you for rescuing me."

"Baking soda," Ms. Bruder said. "Unless you're allergic. Then it's right to the hospital."

"I don't think I'm allergic." Spying the woman's hat, Melanie darted from behind the tree and picked it up. "Here."

Ms. Bruder plopped it on her head, her no-nonsense expression returning. "Now back to business. You need to catch your pony, and I must teach a lesson. We'll have to move to the arena."

"I'll meet you there. I'm sure Trib went back to his stall."

Ms. Bruder strode off toward the others. "While you're by the barns, see if you can find Gus," she called over her shoulder. "He has some wasp spray."

"I will." Melanie headed down the hill, suddenly noticing a throbbing pain in her backside. Grimacing, she rubbed her tailbone. When Trib dumped her, she must have landed on a rock.

As Melanie approached B barn, she could hear the roar of a motor. Rounding the corner, she spotted Miss Perkins, the other camp director, standing by a garden tractor stopped in the middle of the green with its motor idling. Gus was in the tractor seat, leaning on the steering wheel. Beside the tractor, Miss Perkins was gesturing toward the strips of grass he'd obviously been mowing.

The tractor was so noisy that Melanie couldn't hear what Perky was saying to the groundskeeper. But Gus looked so grumpy, she doubted Miss Perkins was complimenting him.

When the director abruptly strode off, Melanie cupped her hands around her mouth. "Gus!" she hollered, then waved her arms, trying to attract his attention.

Finally noticing her, he shut off the tractor motor. "What?"

"Ms. Bruder needs you to spray the warm-up field for yellow jackets."

Lifting his John Deere cap, he wiped the sweat from his brow with a red handkerchief. "The whole field?"

"No. The nest is in the ground by—" Melanie tried to remember where it was, but it had all happened so fast.

With a snort of annoyance, Gus climbed off the tractor.

"I'll find it," he said as he walked stiff-legged over to the equipment shed in back of B barn.

"Thanks," Melanie said, then limped across the green and down the aisle of A barn. The morning had been such a disaster, she wouldn't have been surprised if Trib had run into town instead of his stall.

The stall door was open. She looked inside, spying the pony's familiar white-and-black rump. But her sigh of relief turned into a groan of dismay when she also saw Dana.

The junior instructor stood at Trib's head. "What is the meaning of this?" she asked, holding up his reins. The leather had snapped in two. "I heard a commotion, and came out of Fantasia's stall to see Trib trot down the aisle. He obviously stepped on his rein and broke it."

Melanie opened her mouth to explain, but Dana cut her off. "A most dangerous situation that will be reported to *Ms. Bruder.*"

Dana put such emphasis on the name that it was obvious it was supposed to send chills up Melanie's spine.

"Go ahead," she said coolly, jerking the reins from Dana's grasp. "And while you're at it, tell her that Gus is on his way."

For a second, Dana looked surprised. But then she turned and marched from the stall. Melanie didn't even bother to stick her tongue out. Let Dana find out for herself what had happened. The yellow jackets were hardly her fault.

19

She inspected the reins. Since they had snapped unevenly, she wouldn't be able to use them. Fortunately, Melanie knew that Christina had a pair of spare reins in her trunk for just such an emergency.

She found them, attached them to Trib's bit, then led him from the stall. In the middle of the green, Trib balked. Melanie knew how he felt, and for a second, she thought about forgetting the lesson, too.

It was hot and she was tired. Her tailbone, cheek, and neck throbbed. But she knew she had to get back to the lesson. She'd messed up big-time this morning, and it might be the only way to keep her team from losing even more points. Even if she didn't care about winning, she knew that they did.

"Come on Trib," she urged. "I promise I'll bring you a whole bag of carrots."

Trib only rolled his eyes. Finally, after whacking him on the rear with her palm, Melanie got him going, and reluctantly, the two headed up the hill.

An hour later, when the lesson was over, Melanie collapsed in the saddle. Now she knew why the campers who'd previously been at Saddlebrook had warned everybody about Frieda Bruder. She'd made them practice sitting trots and halts the entire lesson. Melanie's arms and legs were numb.

Dismounting gingerly, she pulled the reins over Trib's head. As she started down the hill, Ms. Bruder came over. "Did you put baking soda on your stings?" the instructor asked, walking beside her.

Melanie shook her head. "I think they'll be fine. They're starting to itch already."

"Good sign." Ms. Bruder smiled, then angled off toward the house.

By the time Melanie led Trib down the hill, the other campers in A barn had their horses untacked.

"You okay?" Christina asked when Melanie passed Sterling's stall. She had a bucket in one hand and was opening her trunk.

"Yeah," Melanie said. "Only Trib broke his reins and I had to borrow your spare pair."

"That's okay. . . . Hey!" Christina blurted. "What did you do to my trunk?"

"What do you mean?" Melanie stopped Trib in the aisle.

Crouching in front of the opened trunk, Christina was rummaging through it. "You messed it up. Nothing's where it's supposed to be."

Melanie gulped. She didn't remember messing anything up. In fact, the reins had been on top in plain sight.

"But I didn't mess it up," Melanie said. Leading Trib closer, she peered over Christina's shoulder. Her cousin was right. It was as if someone had picked up the huge trunk and shook it.

"And look at this!" Christina continued. "You dropped crumbs from your stupid granola bar everywhere. They're stuck on my leg wraps, my bandages, and they're all over the bottom. I'm going to have to dump the whole thing out and start over."

"But I didn't even eat a granola bar when I was in your trunk," Melanie protested.

Standing up, Christina stared at Melanie. "Then who did? You're the only one who has granola bars, and you were in my trunk last."

"True, but I didn't do it!"

Christina plopped her hands on her hips. "Then how do you explain the fact that the trunk was fine before I left for the lesson, and you were the only one who came back here. Everybody else was riding all morning."

"I-I-. I-I-," Melanie sputtered. Christina was right. She couldn't explain it. "I have no idea."

"That's what I thought," Christina said, and picking up her bucket she strode across the green to the water spigot.

"Hey!" Melanie hurried after her, Trib in tow. "Why would I want to mess up your trunk?"

Christina whirled. "Because you didn't want to be the only one who totally blew it this morning. This way when our team only earns a few lousy points, it won't be all your fault."

Melanie's mouth fell open. How could her cousin accuse her of such a devious plan?

Suddenly, she realized half the campers had stopped what they were doing to stare at her. Melanie shrugged her shoulders, trying to pretend that it was no big deal. But when she led Trib into the stall, she sagged against the wall and tears pricked her eyes.

She knew why Christina could accuse her of messing up her trunk. It sounded exactly like something Melanie would have cooked up when she first arrived in Kentucky. When she first met Christina, the two girls hadn't liked each other very much.

But that wasn't true anymore, and Melanie hadn't wrecked her cousin's stuff.

Now she just had to prove it to Christina.

WHEN TRIB WAS FINALLY COOL AND DRY, MELANIE WENT UP to the house for lunch. The old Victorian farmhouse had a kitchen, two dining areas, an office, and bedrooms upstairs for Jody—one of the senior instructors, Miss Perkins, and Ms. Bruder.

Melanie was intentionally late, hoping to avoid the nosy stares of the other campers. The shady porch was deserted except for Sean who was sitting in the swing. His shaggy, blond hair was plastered to his head with sweat and his face was red from the heat, but at least he smiled a greeting.

"What happened to you?" he asked as she clomped up the steps and onto the wooden porch. "Are you auditioning for a monster movie?"

Melanie touched her cheek. She'd almost forgotten about it. "Yeah. 'Return of the Giant Killer Bees.'"

He laughed. "I heard Bruder swept you up in her arms in a daring rescue. Sorry I missed it."

"Believe me, you didn't miss a thing." With a sigh, Melanie plopped down next to him on the swing and pushed off. It swayed gently, and the rush of air felt good against her face.

"It must be a hundred degrees today," she said.

"At least."

They rocked in silence. From inside the house came the clank of plates and the chatter of the campers. Melanie couldn't hear what they were saying, but they were probably talking about her. Maybe she'd skip lunch.

Her stomach growled.

"Aren't you going to eat?" Sean asked.

"Aren't you?"

He shrugged. "I'm hungry, but I need a break from my teammates."

Scraping her boot heels along the floor of the porch, Melanie stopped the swing. "You too?"

"Yeah. Since the quadrille, they're all blaming me for being in fourth place."

"Wow." Melanie blew out her breath. "I thought I was the only one on everybody's hate list."

Just then the screen door burst open. Dylan strolled out carrying a plate of food in his hand. "Too hot in there," he said, sitting down on the steps. "At least there's a slight breeze out here."

Melanie eyed the thick sandwich he'd made, and

her mouth began to water. "So Dylan, how come you're giving Sean such a hard time?" she asked.

Dylan stopped in the middle of a bite. "What are you talking about?" he asked as he lowered his sandwich.

Abruptly, Sean stood up. "She's not talking about anything, Dylan. Sorry I said something to you, *Melanie,*" he added angrily, and he stomped across the porch and went into the house.

"What was that all about?" Dylan asked her.

"Uh, I think I said something Sean didn't want me to. He said that you, Bekka, and Rachel are giving him a hard time about the quadrille."

Dylan looked puzzled. "That's news to me. We all agreed to use music so messing it up wasn't his fault. In fact, Bekka blames herself because Poko cantered so slow."

"Well, he sure is down about something."

"That's easy to figure. It's his parents. He really wanted to impress them Sunday. Obviously, coming in last wasn't what he had in mind."

"Right. I remember hearing them tell him how disappointed they were at the picnic." Dylan took a huge bite of his sandwich. Melanie couldn't stand it any longer. She jumped off the swing. "Well, I better go in and apologize for not keeping my big mouth shut."

"Hey, I'm glad you said something to me," Dylan mumbled, his mouth full. "I'll make sure Sean knows we're not mad at him."

Melanie pulled her boots off, then went into the house. Christina was coming out, a soda can in her hand. She barely even glanced at her.

Great, Melanie thought as she stopped in front of the wash sink. By the end of the day, no one would be speaking to her.

When she turned on the water, she caught sight of her face in the mirror. Her left cheek was puffed out as if she had the mumps and her neck was bright red. With her short, blond hair sticking up in punkish spikes, she looked like a freak.

Melanie blew out a disgusted breath. At least things couldn't get any worse. She turned off the water and pulled a paper towel from the holder.

"Did you see when Trib's saddle slipped and Melanie almost fell off?"

Melanie heard Anita's voice coming from the dining area. Holding her breath, she strained to listen.

"Yeah. I just hope Dana didn't see her." That was Jennifer. "If she did, she'll take off points. Just what our team doesn't need."

"Actually it was pretty funny," Anita said.

At least *she* has a sense of humor, Melanie thought.

"That's easy for you to say," Jennifer shot back. "Melanie's not on your team."

Thanks, Jennifer, Melanie wanted to shout down the hall. Instead she wadded up the paper towel, threw it in the trash, then slammed back outside. There was no way she was going in to eat. She'd just have to starve.

28

"A treat today, ladies and gents," Miss Perkins said in her crisp voice. The director stood in the middle of the porch holding a clipboard in her hand. Frieda Bruder stood behind her.

It was after lunch and campers and instructors were sprawled everywhere. Melanie sat by herself, perched on the porch railing. Glancing sideways, she glimpsed her teammates—Christina, Eliza, and Jennifer—sitting cozily together on the porch swing.

"Because it's so hot today," Miss Perkins continued, "we're going to wait and have lessons this evening when it's cooler."

"Yay!" Cheers rang around the porch.

"Mrs. Henderson is fixing a light, early dinner scheduled for five-thirty. Have your horses groomed, so all you need to do is saddle up. Lessons will be at six-thirty."

"So what do we do all afternoon?" Bekka asked. She was stick-thin with curly, red hair.

"Listen to a boring lecture," Sean whispered loud enough for several people to hear and start laughing.

Miss Perkins smiled. "No boring lectures. Gus has agreed to ferry several van-fulls to the community pool."

"The pool!"

"Yes!"

"It's about time we had fun!"

Melanie felt totally relieved. A reprieve from riding and points would be great and the cool water would feel heavenly on her stings.

Miss Perkins rapped her pen on her clipboard. "Attention please!" When the group quieted, she turned to Ms. Bruder. "I would like to formally introduce Frieda Bruder, though I realize some of you have already met her." She smiled at Melanie, and everybody laughed.

"Way to ride that bucking bronco, Mel!" Anita called across the porch, and several kids whistled and cheered. Melanie couldn't help but join in, even if it was embarrassing.

"Ms. Bruder is a former Olympic rider. Currently, she is much in demand as a dressage-show judge. We are fortunate she will be teaching this week as well as judging Saturday's dressage competition. Please welcome her."

Ms. Bruder stepped forward and everyone clapped. "Thank you for that rousing greeting," the older woman said. "I'm sure by the end of the week, you won't be quite so happy to see me. I have a reputation as a tough taskmaster."

Nervous chuckles and murmurs spread around the porch. After this morning's lesson, Melanie knew she was telling the truth.

"But by next Saturday, you and your mounts will be ready for the dressage test," Ms. Bruder added. "Now off to get your bathing suits. The first van to the pool leaves in twenty minutes."

Everybody scrambled to their feet. Melanie jumped off the porch railing. When Christina walked past, Melanie touched her shoulder. "Can I talk to you?"

"Sure, Cuz." Melanie was glad to see that her cousin's smile was friendly. Going down the stairs, they fell into step together.

"Still mad at me?" Melanie asked.

"Nah." Christina smiled sweetly. *Too* sweetly, Melanie thought warily. Suddenly, Christina's arm whipped around. She had a squirt gun in her hand. "Don't get mad, get even!" she whooped, blasting Melanie in the face.

"You creep!" Melanie lunged for her, but Christina was too fast. Giggling wildly, she raced up the hill to the kennels, disappearing around the corner of the building.

Scowling, Melanie wiped the water off her face. Behind her, several kids on the porch laughed.

"Starting your swim early?" Nathan Hitchcock asked as he walked past. He was a tall, lanky eighteen-year-old and one of the other senior instructors.

"Yup." Melanie smiled brightly, trying to pretend she thought it was funny, too. But inside, she was boiling. Christina was deliberately making a fool of her in front of everybody.

When Melanie reached the room she shared with Eliza, Jennifer, and Christina, she peered cautiously around the doorjamb, poised for another attack. But the room was empty. Cautiously, Melanie stepped inside. Rummaging through her footlocker at the end of the bunks, she found her bathing suit stuffed between her sneakers. She hadn't brought a beach towel, so she'd have to use the one she used for showers.

She fished her flip-flops from under the bottom bunk, then headed to the bathroom, which was a separate building behind the kennels. Two girls were in the stalls talking back and forth. Melanie could tell by their voices it was Bekka and Anita. "I can't wait to swim!" Bekka was saying.

Setting her towel on one of the sinks, Melanie tuned the two girls out. She wished it was she and Christina or Eliza or Jennifer talking excitedly about the pool. Instead, her teammates seemed to have it in for her.

Especially Christina. Melanie thought she and her cousin had become good friends. But if Christina had been a real friend, she wouldn't be accusing Melanie of trashing her trunk.

Melanie looked at her grumpy face in the mirror over the sink. "You are taking this whole thing too seriously," she muttered to her image.

But she knew why. The incident brought back bad memories. She couldn't help but think about Aynslee, her so-called friend in New York. Not only had Aynslee turned into a liar, but she'd abandoned Melanie when she'd needed her the most.

Picking up her suit, Melanie turned away from the sink. Bekka and Anita were still in the stalls changing. Bending down, Melanie peeked under the door of the third stall. It was empty.

She pushed open the door. Christina was standing on the toilet seat, the squirt gun aimed right at Melanie.

"Gotcha!" she said triumphantly as a stream of

water hit Melanie in the forehead. Throwing up her hands, Melanie stumbled backward. The water spurted onto her suit, soaking the nylon material.

With a devilish laugh, Christina jumped off the toilet. "Now we're even!"

"Only I didn't do anything to you!" Melanie shouted, tears filling her eyes.

Christina's smile died. "Hey, don't get so freaked. I was just having fun."

"Fun!" Melanie retorted. "Making a fool out of me is fun?"

Just then Bekka and Anita came out of the stalls dressed in their bathing suits. Smiling awkwardly, they grabbed their stuff and left hurriedly.

Brushing the water and tears from her face, Melanie turned her back to Christina. She didn't want her cousin to see her crying.

"Mel." Christina touched her on the shoulder. "I *was* just playing. Really." Her tone was so sincere, Melanie realized she meant it. Melanie was the one who had overreacted.

"At first I was a little mad about the trunk," Christina continued. "Then I decided it was kind of funny, and Dana never saw it so it didn't matter."

"Oh," Melanie whispered, suddenly feeling stupid. "I thought you were really ticked off and this was your way of getting back at me."

"No." Christina shook her head vehemently. "Look, not only are we cousins, but we're friends. I'm sorry if I embarrassed you. I guess squirting you was pretty stupid, huh."

"*Really* stupid," Melanie agreed solemnly. "I just wish I'd thought of it first." She tried to grab the squirt gun, but Christina was too quick. The girls burst out laughing.

"I'm going to change into my suit, too," Christina said as she headed for the exit. "I want to get out of this place and go swimming."

"See you at the van." When Christina left, Melanie breathed a sigh of relief. Thank goodness everything was okay. She never should have compared Christina with Aynslee.

Going into the stall, she hung her suit on the peg. As she started to pull off her T-shirt, it suddenly dawned on her that everything *wasn't* okay.

True, Christina wasn't mad at her anymore, but she still thought Melanie had messed up her trunk. Melanie had to catch up to her cousin and make her understand once and for all that she didn't do it.

Leaving her things in the bathroom, she jogged down the path to the kennels. Christina wasn't in their room, but she heard voices coming from the room Bekka, Anita, Poe, and Dana shared.

"What's going on?" Melanie asked as she opened the screen door.

Four pairs of eyes turned to stare at her. Anita, Bekka and Christina stood to one side. Dana stood next to the bunk bed.

"Someone was in our room," Dana said. "Whoever it was dumped straw on my bed." She pointed to the bottom bunk. The blanket was covered with yellow stalks.

"Who would do that?" Melanie asked.

Dana frowned. "Someone who really hates me, I guess."

That could be anyone, Melanie thought, but then she noticed the way Dana was glaring at her. "Wait a minute. You guys don't think it was me, do you?" she asked as she glanced from girl to girl.

Anita shrugged, Bekka looked at her bare feet, and Christina's face reddened. Only Dana met Melanie's gaze, and her eyes were definitely accusing.

Melanie opened her mouth to protest, then slowly closed it. What was the use? If her own cousin didn't believe her about the trunk, she knew Dana wouldn't believe her about the straw. Without a word, she turned and ran from the room letting the screen door bang shut behind her.

"FORGET SWIMMING," MELANIE MUTTERED AS SHE HURRIED to the bathroom to retrieve her suit. She'd rather spend the afternoon in a hot dorm with a book than in a pool with a bunch of sharks.

"Mel!" Christina called. Melanie glanced over her shoulder. Her cousin was jogging after her. Without slowing, Melanie strode up the hill and into the bathroom.

"Wait a second." Christina caught up before Melanie could escape into a stall. "No one was accusing you."

"No one was sticking up for me either."

"I know. But what could I say? 'Gee, Dana, since *everybody* hates you, that means any of us could have trashed your bed.'"

"Yes, that's exactly what you should have said," Melanie replied hotly, then started laughing.

"You're right." Christina giggled along with her. "Now come on, let's get ready before the van leaves."

Melanie's expression turned serious. "Not until you understand one thing—I did *not* mess up your trunk. And I did not put straw on Dana's bed."

"For sure?"

"For sure."

"Cross your heart?"

"Cross my heart."

"Wow." Frowning, Christina leaned back against the sink. "Then who do you think did?"

Melanie shook her head. "I have no idea unless—" An idea popped into her head.

"Unless what?" Christina prompted.

"Unless it was Dana. I was wrong when I said I was the only one at the barn during lessons. Dana was there, too. When Trib dumped me and ran back to the barn, she was in Fantasia's stall."

"But why would Dana trash my trunk?"

"Isn't it obvious? She wants our team to lose. She's always hunting for specks of dust in the aisle or teensy grass stains on our bits so she can take off points."

Christina didn't look convinced. "I don't know, Mel. Dana's not devious, just really picky."

"Just picky?" Melanie stared at her in disbelief. She knew how mean Dana had been to Christina when they'd first arrived.

"Okay, she's obnoxious, too. Still, I can't see her deliberately sabotaging my trunk. And why would she put straw on her own bed? There must be another explanation."

"I can think of only one other explanation." Putting a finger to her lips, Melanie whispered, "It's the Ghost of Saddlebrook."

Christina's hazel eyes widened. "The Ghost of Saddlebrook?"

"Yes. Five years ago, a young camper died mysteriously," Melanie said, her voice low and dramatic. "Some people say that Frieda Bruder worked her to death. That's why she haunts Saddlebrook—to warn us about sitting trots."

"Mel!" Laughing, Christina punched her lightly on the arm. "You are a jerk."

"That's me." Picking up her towel and suit, Melanie went into the stall to change. "But if Dana didn't do it, then it had to be the ghost."

"Sure." Still laughing, Christina said good-bye.

Melanie latched the stall door behind her, then unzipped her sweaty breeches. After talking to Christina, she felt a hundred times better. As long as her cousin believed her, it didn't matter what Dana, Anita, or the other campers thought.

The Ghost of Saddlebrook. Melanie grinned as she changed into her bathing suit. Christina had almost fallen for her story. Too bad there wasn't a ghost. At least it would explain who had messed up Christina's trunk and Dana's bed.

The sudden slam of the screen door made Melanie

jump. Wondering who had come into the bathroom, she peeked through the crack between the door and the frame, but couldn't see anything. Bending, she peered under the door. She couldn't see any legs, either.

"Hello," she called.

Her echoed "hello" was the only answer. Quickly, she gathered her clothes and flung open the door. The bathroom was empty.

That's strange. Had the wind slammed the door? Or was her own goofy story freaking her out?

Shivers raced up Melanie's bare arms. She really didn't want to hang around and find out the answer. Grabbing her towel from the counter, she hurried from the bathroom. Outside the door, she found a pen lying in the scuffed dirt. Curious, she picked it up. FRANK'S HARDWARE was written on it.

She knew it hadn't been there when she'd entered the bathroom. Had someone followed her and Christina up the hill? Had they hovered outside the door, listening in on their conversation?

Twirling the pen in her fingers, Melanie headed slowly back to the kennels. She couldn't believe someone would spy on them. Still, she couldn't shake off the feeling that someone had been sneaking around outside the bathroom.

And it wasn't the Ghost of Saddlebrook.

*   *   *

"Hold still, Trib," Melanie said. She was crouched by the pony's front legs, buckling on his protective boots. Everyone from Christina to Miss Perkins had told her how important it was to make sure the boots weren't too loose or too tight so Melanie wanted to get them just right.

"There." She stood up and inspected her work. This evening they were schooling over the cross-country course. They had jumped individual fences before, but tonight they were putting together a small course.

And Melanie was nervous.

Trib loved to run. And usually when he ran, he bucked. The two were doing great together in the jumping ring and dressage arena, but Melanie knew it would be tough to control Trib when they galloped across the fields. She'd already gotten dumped once today. Twice would not be any fun.

Melanie rubbed her bottom. When she'd changed into her clothes after swimming, she'd noticed a big bruise where she'd landed. Doing a cannonball into the pool hadn't helped either. At least the water had made her yellow-jacket stings feel better. Her cheek wasn't as swollen, though it still itched.

"Ready, Mel?" Christina and Sterling poked their heads over the stall door. Sterling blew excitedly at Trib and the pony nickered a greeting.

"I guess." Melanie tried to sound enthusiastic. Christina didn't need to hear about her troubles. She had enough to worry about with Sterling. The Thoroughbred mare had only been off the racetrack since spring and needed lots of work.

Christina backed Sterling away from the door. "I'm really excited," she said. She wore a red safety vest, the same color as Sterling's splint boots. "This is what I've been waiting for. Forget trotting over endless cavalletti. I'm dying to race across the cross-country course, the wind whipping against my cheeks as I leap Trakehners and zig-zags."

"Me too," Melanie muttered as she led Trib from the stall. She didn't have a clue what Trakehners and zig-zags looked like, except they sounded big and dangerous. Stopping in the aisle, she pulled her blue vest from her trunk.

"You don't sound too excited," Christina said.

Melanie slipped the vest over her head, then smoothed down the Velcro fasteners on the sides. "I just don't want to get dumped again."

"Why don't you ask Jody what to do when Trib gets too strong," Christina suggested. "Actually, I need to know, too." She smiled a little nervously. "You know Sterling."

Melanie looked at her cousin in surprise. Was she a little scared, too? Christina was a great rider and she always acted like she could handle anything. Plus, eventing was her big dream. She'd even ridden Sterling cross-country not long after fracturing her wrist.

Still, Sterling had thrown Christina more than once, and the mare had a bad reputation for balking at water.

42

A few sessions in the stream had helped, but Melanie knew how unpredictable horses could be—especially flighty Thoroughbreds.

And knuckleheaded ponies, she added to herself as she scratched Trib under his forelock.

"Good idea," Melanie agreed. "Jody or Nathan should know what to do."

After putting on her helmet, Melanie was ready. She was also a hundred degrees under the hot vest. She was glad they'd waited to ride in the evening. Even though the sun hadn't gone down yet, it was still cooler than the afternoon.

As they led their horses up the hill to the warm-up field, they were joined by several of the other campers. Melanie was glad to see that Anita and her pony, Mushroom, and Poe and her chubby horse, Pork Chop, were in their group. If they could get around the course, so could she.

"Hurry up, guys!" Jody called from the top of the hill. She was mounted on her Hanoverian mare, Queen of Hearts. Queenie was big and gorgeous and probably the most experienced event horse at the camp. Beside her stood Bekka holding Poko, her Appaloosa, and Dana mounted on her bay Morgan mare, Fantasia.

"I don't see Rachel," Christina said as they got closer.

"She's with Sean and Dylan's group," Anita said.

"She's moved up with the hotshots?" Melanie asked, surprised. Rachel didn't seem to be any better than the rest of them.

Anita shrugged. "I guess. Nymph is pretty athletic over fences."

Melanie glanced at Christina who was biting her lip and scowling. Melanie knew Christina wanted to be with the more experienced riders. But since Sterling was so green, Miss Perkins had kept her with the novice group. Plus, she knew Christina wasn't excited about Rachel and Dylan spending even more time together.

When the campers reached Jody, she told them to mount up. "We don't have much time before the sun goes down. Then it will be too spooky to jump. We'll warm up with a brisk trot to the cross-country course."

"Maybe it'll be so spooky, we'll see the Ghost of Saddlebrook," Melanie whispered to Christina, hoping to make her cousin smile.

"What?" Poe overheard. "A ghost?"

"Don't tell me you haven't heard of the Ghost of Saddlebrook!" Christina said in mock seriousness.

Dana looked at the girls with a disgusted expression. "I've been at camp three years and never once heard of the Ghost of Saddlebrook."

"That's because the ghost only reveals herself to great riders," Melanie said.

"Give me a break," Dana scoffed. Clucking to Fantasia, she steered her over toward Jody.

"Uh oh, you made her mad now," Christina said.

"So what else is new." Suddenly, Melanie thought about the pen from Frank's Hardware. Dana was always carrying a pen around, tapping her clipboard or chewing on the end while she decided how many points to knock off.

"You guys are just teasing about the ghost, right?" Poe asked. She'd been struggling to mount Pork Chop, but the horse's withers were so fat and round that the saddle kept slipping.

"Right." Melanie went around to Pork Chop's right side. "Here let me hold the other stirrup for you." She held onto the stirrup, keeping the saddle from tipping while Poe mounted.

"Thanks," Poe said, and after checking her girth, she rode after Christina who'd joined Jody and the others.

Trib swung around to go with them. "Whoa. Stand," Melanie said in her firmest voice. Gathering the reins, she stuck her toe in the stirrup. Trib tossed his head and pranced sideways. Melanie barely made it into the saddle before he took off at a bouncy trot.

Gritting her teeth, she pulled him to a halt. He chewed on the bit, tossed his head and switched his tail. But she forced him to stand until she'd gotten both feet in the stirrups.

Only then did she let him head after the others. Breaking into a canter, he quickly caught up, charging past Queenie before slowing to a trot.

"Having problems?" Jody asked with a smile.

Melanie caught her breath. "Yes! Trib is such a brat."

Jody laughed. "He is Mr. Spunky."

45

"Spunky would be great if this was a personality contest." Melanie wiped off the sweat that had trickled from under her hot helmet. "But I'm afraid he's going to take off with me cross-country."

"I've got something that might help."

"You do?" Melanie exhaled with relief. "Oh, thank you! Thank you."

"Don't thank me unless it works." Jody halted Queenie beside the first cross-country fence—a stack of telephone poles that looked ten-feet high. Melanie halted Trib in front of it. He could barely see over the top.

"We're going to canter up the hill, across the field and down the logging road. As we warm up, I want you to practice rating your horses, that means slowing them to a trot and speeding them up into a hand gallop. They'll want to keep up with me, so you're going to have to be the boss."

Melanie raised her hand. "Only I've got a pony who wants to be the boss."

Jody nodded. "For horses like Sterling, who are off the track, and hard-headed ponies like Trib, I suggest you practice using a bridge."

Jody demonstrated how to hold both reins in each hand. Then she wedged her fists securely on each side of Queenie's neck. "A bridge keeps your hands steady and your body balanced. If you stay balanced, you have better control. Practice using it as we canter."

"Uh, I've got the opposite problem with Pork Chop," Poe said. "He'd rather fall asleep—"

Melanie didn't hear the rest of what Poe said because Dana steered Fantasia between Trib and Pork Chop. The junior instructor had a smirk on her face. "So, Mel, what I can't figure out is how come *you* saw the ghost," Dana said. "You're the worst rider at camp."

"I guess the ghost didn't think so," Melanie said, refusing to let Dana get her goat. "Oh, by the way. Did you lose your pen? The one that said 'Frank's *Under-wear*' on it?"

"*Hardware*," Dana retorted. "That's my dad's business. And yes, I did lose it. Where'd you find it?"

"Outside the bathroom door." Melanie kept a straight face.

Dana's cheeks flushed. "Oh, I must have dropped it when I changed. I'll get it later tonight. Thanks," she added before turning Fantasia and riding quickly off.

Gotcha. Melanie had to press her lips together to keep from grinning triumphantly. Dana *had* been outside the door. And Melanie bet she'd been listening to every word.

But why would Dana want to spy on the two girls? Was she the prankster? Had she trashed her own bed just to get Melanie in trouble?

A creepy feeling prickled up Melanie's arms. What if Dana disliked her so much she'd do anything to make Melanie look bad? And if that were the case, what would Dana do next?

5

I've got to tell Christina. Swinging around in the saddle, Melanie looked for her cousin. Christina was on the other side of Jody, talking to Anita.

"Come on, Trib." Melanie jogged the pony toward Sterling, but before they reached Christina, Jody hollered, "Let's go, campers."

Turning Queenie, Jody headed toward the woods at a brisk trot. Immediately, Trib broke into a canter. Startled, Melanie plopped forward onto the pony's neck. When the terrain leveled out, Melanie could feel the pony pick up speed. Cantering beside Sterling, he ducked his head and humped his back.

Uh oh. Melanie knew what that meant. He was getting ready to buck. She grimaced. The last thing she needed was to fall off again.

Quickly, she pulled up his head. Grabbing both reins with each hand, she made a bridge across his neck.

Then she shoved her heels down and using her legs like shock absorbers, she sat deeper.

Slowly, his canter smoothed. Instead of bobbing and bouncing, Melanie rocked rhythmically in the saddle. The wind whistled in her ears and blew warm against her cheeks.

Glancing sideways, Melanie grinned at Christina. Her cousin grinned back. Sterling's ears were pricked and her dapples sparkled in the sunlight.

The group thundered into the dusky woods and, two abreast, cantered down the logging road. For a second, Melanie felt as if she and Trib were flying. The exhilaration sent goosebumps up her arms.

This was what riding was all about!

In the lead, Jody raised one arm, signaling the others to slow down. Trib automatically broke into a trot. He was puffing and his neck was sweaty.

"Wow! That was totally cool!" Melanie gasped when they halted.

"Totally," Christina agreed. Her face was flushed and Sterling, still eager to go, danced sideways. Steering Trib over to the mare, Melanie held her reins in one hand and raised the other. Christina leaned over and the two slapped palms while shouting, "Awesome!"

When the campers rode their horses into the woods, Melanie made sure Dana was out of earshot, then told Christina about the pen.

"Do you really think Dana's out to get us?" Christina whispered.

Melanie shrugged. "It's the only thing that makes sense. I think she wants our team to lose."

"Maybe Dylan's team is paying her off," Christina suggested, giggling, and Melanie knew she wasn't taking it seriously. But then she wasn't being accused of the pranks, either.

The logging road through the woods led to the outskirts of a hilly field. Five jumps dotted the field: two fairly close by, three down near a wide stream. On the other side of the stream were more woods and beyond that, in the distance, Melanie could see the wavy, gray-blue line of the mountains.

Melanie had never been this far from the main camp before, and it was beautiful. Whitebrook Farm was pretty, too, but not as wild. Growing up in New York City, she'd seen lots of Broadway shows and art exhibits, but very few wide-open spaces.

Jody stopped next to the first jump—three six-foot-long logs laid end to end. The first log was about a foot high, the second about two-feet high and two-feet wide, and the third was so huge, Melanie figured Paul Bunyan must have chopped it down.

"Here's the drill," Jody said. "You're going to ride a course of six obstacles. But first, we'll walk around and discuss how to approach each one."

"Very carefully," Melanie said, and everybody laughed.

Jody gestured toward the one-foot log. "You will be jumping the smallest section of each fence. The ones on the left."

Several cheers went up. Melanie heard Christina grumble something about "baby fences."

"And remember," Jody continued. "Red flag on your right. White flag on your left."

Melanie twisted in her saddle to check out the flags. They weren't really flags, she realized, but triangle-shaped, wooden markers.

The next fence looked like a lightning bolt made of thick poles. "This is a zig-zag," Jody explained. "It isn't hard to jump, but it can confuse the horse. You should jump the point going *toward* you," she emphasized. "That way, if you make a mistake, your horse won't land on the back point."

"The third obstacle is a bank," Jody called over her shoulder as she rode down the hill, the riders behind her. "Stay to the left. The drop is a little over three feet which is consistent with a novice test. If you make a mistake and go right, the drop is almost five feet."

Melanie grimaced. "Remember that, Trib. No ducking to the right or you'll have a big surprise."

"Take the bank at a trot, then trot or canter across the stream. The footing is firm." Jody guided Queenie into the slow-moving water.

Trib splashed eagerly after her. The water reached his knees and almost touched the stirrups. Stopping in the middle, he started to paw. Melanie gave him a sharp kick. Knowing Trib, he'd roll if he got the chance.

As Trib clambered out of the stream, Melanie looked over her shoulder. Sterling stood on the bank on the other side, eyeing the water suspiciously. But when she saw that all the other horses were going to leave her, she tucked her tail and plunged across.

Jody waved her hand toward the woods. A path had been mowed between the tall broomgrass and weeds. "Keep your horse moving forward up the slope. At the top, there're several gates built between the trees. Make sure you jump the left gate—it's about two-feet tall. The one in the middle is three feet, the one on the left is four."

The riders trotted up the path, checked out the gate, and followed the mowed area down the hill. "After the gate, swing right," Jody instructed. "Keep your horse steady because the next obstacle is a bounce jump. Does anyone know what that is?"

"Me!" Melanie waved her arm eagerly. "It's a fence with a mattress on the other side so that when you fall off, you bounce to your feet."

Everybody laughed, including Jody. "Not exactly," the senior instructor said. "Chris?"

Christina had been waving her hand, too. "A bounce is when the horse jumps over the first jump," she explained, "then immediately takes off and jumps the next one with no stride in between."

Jody nodded. "That's correct."

"Show off," Melanie said behind her hand.

"And last," Jody went on, gesturing to the other side of the stream, "canter back through the water, keeping your impulsion, and jump up the bank."

The group rode across the stream to the other side. Jody halted Queenie under the shade of a lone oak. From there, they could see all the jumps. "Who's first?" the instructor asked.

Melanie gulped nervously. She wanted to watch how the others did before she went. No one else volunteered, either. Finally, Christina cleared her throat and said, "I'll go."

"Sterling will be fine," Jody reassured her, but the pinched look on Christina's face told Melanie that her cousin wasn't as confident. "In fact, if she's going well, take her over the middle gate."

Christina nodded, then trotted Sterling to the top of the hill. Melanie held her breath as the duo approached the log. They sailed over it, cantered smoothly to the zig-zag, leaped over it, and headed to the bank.

"Very nice," Jody said. "Christina's keeping the mare at an even pace. Steady now, use your bridge," she shouted as Sterling cantered down the hill.

The mare bounded down over the bank. Melanie could see the determined expression on Christina's face as they approached the stream. Two strides from the edge of the water, Sterling's head flew up, her ears flicked back and forth, and she began to weave.

"Don't stop," Melanie said under her breath.

"Legs! Seat! Push her across!" Jody hollered.

Sitting deep in the saddle, Christina clamped her legs onto Sterling's sides and pumped with her seat. "Come on!" she urged.

The mare hesitated, then charged across the stream. Spray flew everywhere.

"Yay!" Melanie and the others cheered. At the top of the hill, Christina took the middle gate then headed for the bounce. Because Sterling had such a long stride, Melanie knew the bounce might give the mare the most trouble.

But Christina pulled Sterling to a trot, and they cleared it beautifully, Sterling jumping the second fence as if it was four-feet high instead of two.

When she rode up, Christina's face was flushed with heat and excitement, but she was grinning from ear to ear.

"Congratulations, Cuz!" Melanie said. "I thought at first we were going to have to fish you and Sterling out of the stream, but you pulled it off."

"Yes. Very nice, Christina. You've learned a lot," Jody said, which made Christina's cheeks turn even pinker.

"Your turn, Melanie," Jody said.

"Me?" Melanie sputtered. She was not ready to go yet.

"Yup. First the biggest horse, now the spunkiest."

Melanie wrinkled her nose. "How about the fattest?" she suggested. "Then Pork Chop could go next."

"Hey, that's not funny," Poe protested.

"Go on, Melanie," Anita and Bekka chorused.

"All right." Melanie squeezed her heels against Trib's sides and shortened her reins. The pony took two steps, then swatted his tail, and hopped in place, protesting leaving the group.

"Trib," Melanie said in her fiercest I'm-in-charge voice, *"Trot."*

He broke into a reluctant trot. At least he won't run away with me, Melanie thought. But when she turned him toward the log, his pace quickened and his ears flipped forward. One thing Trib loved to do was jump.

And buck, Melanie reminded herself.

The pony leaped the log without hesitation then cantered to the zig-zag. Using her left rein, Melanie guided him to the smallest side. He jumped the point as if he had wings on his feet. Grabbing mane, she held tightly to keep from getting left behind but when he landed, she lost a stirrup.

Losing her balance, she fell forward onto his neck. Her stirrup flopped, her reins went slack.

I'm doomed. The two words flickered through Melanie's numb brain as Trib raced downhill toward the bank. She wanted to throw her arms around his neck, close her eyes, and pray that she'd make it in one piece.

As Trib hurtled down the hill, Melanie could hear Jody hollering something, "Use a pulley rein to . . . then circle until . . ."

Her instructions broke through Melanie's fear. I know what to do, she told herself. *I do!*

Bracing her left hand against his neck, she gripped the right rein firmly and pulled. Trib swung to the right, then circled, heading back up the hill. When his pace slowed, Melanie was able to get her foot in the stirrup.

She regained her balance, used her bridge to get him into an even canter, and once again pointed him to the bank. Dropping down over it, he splashed through the stream and bounded up the hill.

I did it! Melanie thought excitedly, then the gate loomed in front of her and her heart began to pound. She directed her attention on the low left side. *Piece of cake.* But then Trib swerved abruptly and, before Melanie could react, took off over the middle section.

Her cry of whoa died as she felt him arch beneath her and soar effortlessly over the three-foot jump. Landing smoothly, he cantered down the path to the bounce. Melanie couldn't believe she'd hung on. In fact, not only had she hung on, the jump had felt great.

They took the bounce perfectly. In and out and as soon as they were over the second fence, Trib came to a screeching halt as if to say, "Okay, I'm done."

Relieved, yet elated, Melanie let her body go limp. *I did it!* No, *we* did it! She corrected herself, flopped onto Trib's neck, and gave him a big hug.

Half an hour later, the sky was dusky and the group of tired horses and riders ambled back to camp. Melanie was exhausted—her arms and legs felt like Jell-O—but it was a nice kind of exhaustion.

"Boy, I'm ready for a hot shower, clean jammies, a big glass of water, a granola bar and cool sheets,"

Melanie said to Christina who was riding Sterling beside Trib.

Christina snorted. "Don't get too excited. By the time you've finished cooling down Trib, you'll be so tired you'll settle for the cool sheets."

"Oh." Melanie had almost forgotten the horses came first. After bathing, walking, feeding, and wiping off sweaty tack, it would be an hour before she and Christina straggled back to the kennels.

"But it was worth it, right?" Jody commented. She was riding in front of them and must have overheard. "Everybody did a super job."

Melanie glanced over her shoulder at Anita, Poe, Bekka and their horses. They all looked just as tired, but the three girls wore satisfied grins.

"Right," Anita said. "When do we get to do it again?"

"Thursday we'll school over a course of seven more obstacles. That will give you experience over all the jumps for the final cross-country competition next Saturday."

"It will be a course of thirteen?" Poe asked, sounding anxious.

"Right."

"But that's an unlucky number!"

Melanie stifled a giggle and Poe shot her a nasty look. "Don't laugh. You were the one talking about a ghost."

"A ghost!" Anita and Bekka chorused.

"The Ghost of Saddlebrook," Melanie said.

"Haven't you heard of her?" Christina sounded surprised. "Her name was Felicity. She was a camper at Saddlebrook five years ago. One moonlit night, she died mysteriously. Her teammates found her in the barn, dead, with her fingers clutching the reins of her bridle. Now, she haunts the camp, warning everybody about Frieda Bruder."

Melanie squelched a laugh. Christina was really embellishing the story!

"Frieda?" Jody repeated.

"Yes." Christina dropped her voice low, and everyone leaned forward in their saddles to hear. "Frieda had trotted her to death!"

Cries of "Oh, how stupid" and choked giggles rang in the air. But when they rode into the dark woods, the girls' laughter quieted. Dark shadows flickered across the logging road. Limbs creaked and leaves whooshed. Something skittered in the underbrush and Trib tossed his head. Beside him, Sterling snorted anxiously.

"How about a song, guys?" Jody asked cheerfully.

"We can sing, 'Dem bones, dem bones dem dry bones,'" Melanie suggested, booming out the words in a deep voice.

"No way," Anita retorted. "We need something happy. How about 'Jingle Bells'?"

"It's not Christmas," Bekka pointed out.

As the girls argued, Melanie thought about how much she had enjoyed the evening. Thank goodness she hadn't let the morning disasters—getting stung, falling off, and being accused of things she didn't do— get to her.

Thoughts of the upcoming event entered her mind. Now that jumping cross-country wasn't quite so scary, she was looking forward to the two-day competition, even if her father didn't show up.

Still, a stab of sadness hit her. She hadn't seen her father in over a month. They talked often, but that wasn't the same. Would he come? And if he didn't, would she be able to handle the disappointment?

As they rode from the dark woods and into the field, the girls broke into a rousing chorus of "Ninety-nine bottles of pop on the wall . . ." Melanie realized that she didn't have all the answers. After letting out a big sigh, she pushed her father from her mind and joined in the singing.

6

"GET UP SLEEPYHEAD," SOMEONE SHOUTED IN MELANIE'S ear, then the same someone had the nerve to rudely shake her.

Melanie forced one eye open. Christina was peering over the mattress, her face level with hers.

"Get up or you'll be late," Christina repeated before disappearing. Melanie heard the clunk of boots on wood, then saw Christina's head bobbing across the dorm room.

"What time is it?" Melanie asked, yawning.

Breeches flopped onto her face.

"Hey!" Melanie whipped them off. "What're you doing?"

"I already fed Trib for you. I'm not mucking his stall. I ate. Breakfast will be over in ten minutes."

Melanie bolted upright. "Why didn't you wake me earlier?"

"I did. Half an hour ago. You must have fallen back asleep."

Throwing back the covers, Melanie tugged on her breeches. Christina tossed her the T-shirt she'd worn for the last two days. "Phew." She held her nose. "Don't you have any clean ones?"

"No. We better do laundry today." Melanie pulled off her nightshirt and slipped on the T-shirt. "What day is it? Friday? We should have free time after lunch."

"Great. Just what I want to do with my free time." Christina opened the screen door. "I'll see you at the barn."

Melanie jumped from the bunk. She hunted under the lower bed for her paddock boots and yesterday's socks. She'd been so tired last night, she'd dropped her clothes on the floor and fallen into bed. For three days, Frieda had her lesson group practicing sitting trots, half-halts, and three-point position. Every muscle and bone in her body ached. No wonder Felicity had turned into a ghost.

She pulled on her day-old socks, then stuck her feet in her boots without lacing them and clomped from the room. She'd just have time to grab a bagel or muffin before heading to Trib's stall.

The kitchen was almost deserted by the time Melanie came in. Mrs. Henderson, the cook, was scraping leftovers in the sink and Sean was shoveling spoonfuls of eggs into his mouth.

"Morning," Melanie greeted them as she plucked

two muffins from the basket in the middle of the long wooden table. They were blueberry—her favorite.

Still chewing, Sean stood up. "Can't talk," he mumbled. "Gotta get to the barn."

"Me too." Melanie waved to Mrs. Henderson and followed Sean out the door. Sean wore his blond hair long and this morning, it looked fluffy and soft as if it had just been washed. Melanie touched her own short locks. She hadn't had time to comb her hair.

Melanie hurried to keep up with Sean as he leaped down the steps. She hadn't talked to him alone since Monday—the day she'd told Dylan about Sean being upset.

"So, are we still friends?"

"Why wouldn't we be?" He pulled a pair of sunglasses from the back pocket of his breeches and put them on.

"Well, on Monday I thought I said something that I shouldn't have," Melanie explained. "About you being upset with Dylan because your team was upset with you about the quadrille."

"Ancient history."

"Still, I know how lousy parent problems can be."

"What do parents have to do with me being disappointed in the quadrille?" Sean stopped and turned to face her. His eyes were hidden by his dark lenses.

"Everybody heard your mom and dad chew you out."

Sean's jaw tightened, and Melanie wished she could

take back her words. "I mean, hey, believe me, I have plenty of parent problems of my own," she rushed on. "My dad's canceled hundreds of dates with me. And each time it hurts just as much as the first."

Sean didn't respond. Since his expression was masked by his sunglasses, Melanie wasn't sure what he was thinking. Without a word, he started toward the barn again.

"And what's even worse," she babbled on, "I keep hoping it will change. I keep trying to do things to get his attention."

"I know that routine." Sean nodded his head, but didn't slow down as they headed across the lawn. "Only I have an older brother who my parents think is perfect, so nothing I do is ever good enough."

Melanie's brows rose. "Weren't you the lead in the school play? And you play the guitar, and they must know what a super rider you are."

Sean snorted. "According to my parents, that stuff doesn't count. You have to be a basketball or football star to be worth anything."

"That stinks."

Sean shrugged. "I don't let it get to me anymore." He flashed her a cocky grin. "I've found the best thing to do is laugh it off."

Melanie didn't believe him for one second. Since Sunday, she noticed he hadn't been laughing much.

When they reached the barns, Sean cut to the right. "I've got to get Jester tacked up. See you at lunch."

"See you." Melanie headed across the green to the end of A barn. Eliza, Christina, and Jennifer were clustered around the far support post looking at a piece of paper tacked to it.

Oh, great. Melanie groaned. *Points.* "Hey, guys!" she called. "How many points did Dana give us yesterday?"

When the girls turned around, Melanie gulped. Nobody was smiling.

"You mean how many points did Dana give *you*," Eliza said, her hands on her hips.

"And the answer is zero," Jennifer chimed in.

"Zero?" Melanie came up beside them. "Gee, that must be some kind of camp record," she joked.

No one laughed. Even Christina looked slightly disgruntled. "Our team dropped to third place," she said.

Jennifer tapped the paper. "And it's your fault, Melanie. You got zero points because your stall was dirty. Zero because you had a broken rein. Zero because hay was sprinkled all over the aisle. And zero because you were late for the lesson."

Melanie shrugged. "Trib and I are just irresponsible slobs I guess."

Eliza frowned at her. "And you don't care that you're making our team lose?" she asked angrily.

Melanie bristled. "Of course, I care. But my whole life doesn't revolve around winning some stupid end-of-camp trophy. Camp's supposed to be fun—you know, roasting hot dogs and telling ghost stories around a bonfire—not prison."

"Saturday night we're having a hot-dog roast," Christina said brightly as if trying to keep the girls from arguing.

But Melanie was too angry. "Besides, Dana watches me—us—like a hawk. Even if we were perfect, she'd find something wrong. Or she'd make it look as if we did something wrong."

"Melanie thinks Dana messed up my trunk and put the hay on her own bed," Christina said.

Eliza shook her head. "That's a crazy idea. Why would Dana do that?"

"She doesn't want our team to win," Melanie explained. "And she wants to make me look bad. None of us got many points yesterday."

"At least we didn't get zero," Jennifer fumed.

"True, but look at team two." Christina pointed to the four names. "They're not so hot and yet Dana's been pretty fair to them."

Eliza bent to look closer. "More than fair. She didn't take off hardly any points and now they're number two."

"See?" Melanie said. "That proves my point. Dana's playing favorites. So no matter what we do, we're not going to win. You want my advice? From now on, let's just have fun." She grinned invitingly.

Eliza shook her head. "I can't do that if I want to be a junior instructor next year. Sorry." Turning, she went into Flash's stall.

"Me either," Jennifer said before she left.

Melanie turned to Christina. "That leaves you, Cuz."

Christina was chewing a fingernail. "Sorry, Mel. I want to try and win, too, so I have to agree with the others. Even though I think you're right about Dana."

Melanie blew out a breath. "Okay. I'll try harder. I promise." When Christina went down the aisle, Melanie fell into step beside her. "Though couldn't we have a *little* fun?" she pleaded.

Christina laughed. "Like what?"

Melanie leaned closer. "How about playing a prank on Sean and Dylan tonight?"

"I don't know, Mel. If you get caught, you really will get accused of playing the other jokes," Christina pointed out.

"Hey, I keep getting blamed anyway. At least I'll be guilty this time." Shielding her mouth with her hand, Melanie whispered, "Let's sneak into the carriage house and do something goofy, like smear peanut butter on the guys' toothbrushes or hide the toilet paper."

"Ooo. Sounds wicked." As she unlatched Sterling's stall, Christina started to giggle. "But nothing bad, promise?"

"Promise."

At dinner that night, Melanie checked out all the different platters and bowls as they were passed around. When Anita handed her a bowl of peach jam, her eyes brightened. It would be perfect to smear on the guys' combs and brushes. Tomorrow morning, when they preen in front of the mirror, they'll end up with sticky gunk in their hair.

She ladled out several spoonfuls, then took a slice of Cook's homemade bread. Instead of spreading the jam on the bread, she waited until everybody was eating and talking and scooped the jam into an empty margarine container she'd found on the counter.

There. Plan A was accomplished. Now they just had to figure out a way to sneak into the guys' room.

Looking up, Melanie tried to catch Christina's attention. Her cousin was sitting across the table sandwiched between Eliza and Dylan who were having a lively conversation.

"What do you mean someone switched your bridles?" Eliza was asking Anita who was on her other side.

"All the bridles in B barn were mixed up," Anita explained.

Waving his spoon, Sean said, "I got Mushroom's bridle. I was in such a hurry that I started to put the bit in Jester's mouth before I realized it was the wrong bridle."

"I *did* tack up Dakota," Dylan said. "I only noticed it wasn't his bridle when I put the crownpiece over his ears and it was way too small."

Several other campers in B barn chimed in with their stories.

"How'd you get them all sorted out?" Christina asked.

"Not quickly," Poe replied. "We were late for our lesson. Adrianne docked us points." Leaning back, she hollered the last words through the open doorway that led to the dining room where the instructors ate. "And it wasn't fair because it wasn't our fault!"

Grinning, Melanie speared a bite of ham. Maybe it wasn't fair, but it was pretty funny. She wished she'd thought of switching bridles. What a great joke.

"Then whose fault was it?" Jennifer asked. She sat on Melanie's other side. "How'd they get mixed up?"

Dylan shrugged. "We don't know. This afternoon, when we went to tack up, all the bridles were hanging outside the stalls on their hooks where they belonged. They just weren't the right bridles."

"Weird," Christina said, giving Melanie a strange look.

Melanie froze, her fork in the air. Raising her brows, she mouthed, "Why are you looking at me?"

"So who do you think switched them?" Eliza asked.

Good question, Melanie thought as she popped some ham into her mouth.

"Obviously it was someone who wanted teams one and five to lose points," Bekka said. Several heads turned in Melanie's direction. She swallowed her piece of ham whole, almost choking.

"What are you looking at me for?" she asked. "I didn't switch them."

"*Sure*," Poe muttered under her breath, and even though the other kids looked away, Melanie had the distinct feeling that no one believed her.

"Maybe it was the Ghost of Saddlebrook," Anita piped up.

"Not that stupid ghost again," Poe groaned. But it didn't keep Anita from launching into the story that Christina had told, adding her own gory details as she went on.

Melanie tuned her out. She finished eating and gazed at her plate. Why did everybody automatically think she was the one who'd played the pranks? She didn't even care if her team won.

Melanie had clean-up duty, so when dinner was over she helped clear the table. Eliza was the other person cleaning up. Working on the opposite side of the table, Melanie tried to avoid the older girl. Eliza had made it pretty clear she wasn't too happy with her.

Plop. Something gooey landed on Melanie's arm. When she glanced up, Eliza was heading over to the sink, dishes balanced on her arm.

Frowning, Melanie wiped the gunk off with a napkin, then began to stack plates. Splat. A blob of mashed potatoes hit her on her other arm. Swinging around, Melanie caught Eliza in the middle of flinging a second spoonful.

"Hey!" she sputtered.

Eliza laughed. "Sorry, I couldn't help myself."

Melanie eyed her. "I thought you didn't believe in all this silly stuff? You were too busy being perfect."

"I am. But I thought about what you said earlier. Camp should be fun. Besides," she said mischievously, "you deserve it."

"What's that supposed to mean?"

"Someone's got to get you back for all the pranks you've been playing."

"But I'm not playing any!" Melanie insisted.

"Sure." Eliza's tone was playful. Still, Melanie knew the older girl didn't believe her either.

When the table was cleared, Melanie picked up her margarine container and joined the others in the common room. Kids were sprawled in chairs and sofas reading, playing games or watching a video. Christina was playing cards with Dylan and Poe. Sean, Bekka, and Jennifer had set up a backgammon board.

Melanie walked across the room and over to Christina. "You need to come out to the barn," she said. "Uh, remember . . . You were going to help me learn how to braid Trib's mane."

"I was?" Christina looked up from her cards.

"Gin." With a triumphant grin, Poe laid her cards down.

"You won again!" Dylan grumbled.

Melanie held up the margarine tub. "Yeah. I've got rubber bands."

Christina scrambled to her feet. "Oh, right. I was going to show you how to do a Russian braid."

"See you guys later." Dylan waved, his attention already back on the game. Melanie hurried Christina out the door and onto the lighted porch.

"If we're going to sneak into the guys' room, we better do it now," Melanie whispered.

"Where's Nathan?"

"Nathan!" Melanie had forgotten about the senior instructor who also shared the room above the carriage house. "Wait. There he is. On the porch swing with Adrianne."

Both girls turned nonchalantly. The two instructors were rocking in the swing, so engrossed in each other they didn't even notice them.

"Ooo. I think love is blossoming." Christina giggled.

"Let it. This is our chance." The girls hurried down the porch steps. The carriage house was to the right between the big house and the kennels. It was dark except for a dim lightbulb illuminating the steps up to the rooms.

Christina stopped Melanie at the foot of the steps. "Are you sure you want to go through with this? It seems like you're in enough trouble."

"Yes. Now I'm even being accused of switching bridles, so it's about time I played a real joke on somebody." She snickered. "And who better than the guys!" Glancing right and left to make sure no one was watching, Melanie climbed the stairs. The outer door was unlocked.

"So far so good," she whispered to Christina who

was huddled right behind her. They slipped inside. Since neither had been in the carriage house before, it took them a second to get their bearings.

Fortunately, the lights from the house illuminated the interior, so they could find their way around.

"What now?" Christina whispered.

Melanie handed the container to her. "I brought jam."

"Jam?"

"To smear on their combs and stuff."

Christina giggled. "But Dylan's already so sweet."

"Oh, *ple-e-ease.*"

They tiptoed into the bathroom. Melanie glanced out the small window between the toilet and the shower. The window was open to let in the breeze. Since it overlooked the porch, she could see or hear if anyone was coming. "I'll keep lookout."

Christina popped the top off the tub. "Boy, I hope no one catches us."

Suddenly, Melanie heard voices below. She peered out the window. Sean was coming down the porch steps. He turned right and he headed toward the carriage house.

Melanie yelped. "Sean just came out of the house!"

Christina squealed and dropped the container on the sink. Putting her finger to her lips, Melanie crept to the bathroom door. She could hear the steps creak and then the sound of the outside door opening.

Horrified, Melanie swung around. "He's coming in. We've got to hide!"

7

MELANIE GRABBED CHRISTINA'S WRIST AND YANKED HER toward the shower. "In here. Before he sees us."

Melanie pushed back the curtain, and the two girls climbed into the stall. It was narrow and they were smushed together. Melanie could hear Christina's ragged breathing. She could feel the beating of her own frantic heart.

The lights flicked on and a golden glow streamed into the bathroom. If Sean stayed in the bedroom, he probably wouldn't see them. But if he came into the bathroom . . .

Melanie racked her brain, trying to come up with an explanation why they were in the boys' room hiding in the shower. They were cleaning it? Checking out the plumbing?

Dumb. She'd have to tell Sean the truth. Maybe he'd even think it was funny.

The light went out. When the girls heard the door close, they both sighed with relief.

"That was a close one," Melanie said.

"Too close for me," Christina said, her voice tense. "I'm outta here before someone catches us." She threw open the shower curtain and both girls screamed. Sean was standing in the middle of the bathroom, in the dark, staring at them with an expression of disbelief.

"Sean!" Christina put her hand on her chest. "You scared me to death!"

"What do you mean sneaking up on us like that?" Melanie exclaimed.

"Me?" He jabbed his thumb at his chest. "That's my shower you're hiding in."

Melanie grinned sheepishly. "Oh, right. Ha, ha."

"Still, that was pretty low." Christina climbed from the stall. "We could've had heart attacks or something."

"How'd you know we were in there?" Melanie asked.

He pointed to the margarine tub Christina had dropped on the sink. "I came up to get a pack of cards. When I walked past the bathroom, I caught a glimpse of the container." Cocking his head, he eyed Melanie. "I remember you had it in your hand when you left the common room. After all the jokes you've been pulling, I figured something was up."

"Only I haven't . . ." Melanie started to explain about the other pranks, then decided not to bother.

"But I didn't know *you* were behind them, Christina," he said.

76

"I'm not." Christina gave Melanie an accusing look as if it was all her fault. "I only went along with Melanie when she came up with the idea of playing a prank on you and Dylan."

"We weren't going to do anything nasty," Melanie explained.

Sean peered into the container. "Peach jam?"

"'Cause you're both so sweet," Melanie cooed in a fake voice, echoing what Christina had said earlier.

The three of them burst out laughing. Melanie was glad Sean wasn't mad at them.

Sean stuck his finger in the jam and scooped some up. Then he plucked a toothbrush from the holder and began wiping jam on the bristles.

Melanie's jaw dropped, and Christina looked just as surprised. "What are you doing?" she gasped.

"Trashing Nathan's toothbrush." Sean grinned wickedly. "After all, he's as sweet as Dylan and I. Just ask Adrianne."

"Now *that* should make a bonfire," Melanie said Saturday night. The girls from team four were in charge of gathering wood for the campfire. It was after eight, the sun was setting, and Melanie had just piled an armful of dead wood on top of the huge pile.

Jennifer came up beside her and dropped two skinny logs on the ground. Her T-shirt was covered with dirt, and she had scratches on her arms. "All I know is I'm never going camping unless there's electricity."

"Marshmallows roasted over a stove aren't quite the same," Melanie said, laughing.

"Is this enough?" Christina grumbled as she and Eliza came out of the woods dragging several branches. When she saw the stack of wood, she answered her own question. "Definitely."

Wiping her brow on her sleeve, Eliza plopped down on a round log they'd decided to use for a seat. "I think we got the worst job."

"That's because Dana was in charge," Melanie reminded her. "She gave Dylan's team the cushy job of finding sticks to put the marshmallows and hot dogs on."

"And team two's making cookies," Jennifer chimed in.

"Yum." Christina licked her lips. She glanced down at her own dirty T-shirt. "I'm going to change before the big bonfire."

"Ooo, hoping *Dylan* will sit next to you?" Melanie teased as she headed to the kennels with her.

"So did you see Nathan at breakfast this morning?" Melanie asked Christina as they walked from the barn. "He looked mad—and wet."

Christina grinned. "Dylan said he had to wash his hair twice to get the jam out."

"You didn't tell Dylan we were in the carriage house, did you?"

"No way. And if Sean keeps his mouth shut, no one should find out, either."

"Good, I don't need Nathan mad at me, too," Melanie said.

Later, when the girls returned to the campfire, the sky was dark and the fire was crackling merrily. A half-dozen campers were sitting around on blankets or logs. Gus stood beside the fire with a stick in one hand to poke the embers. On the ground, he'd laid a hose which wound toward the tractor shed.

Melanie spread out the blanket she and Christina had brought. At the same time, Miss Perkins and Ms. Bruder arrived with most of the other campers. The directors' arms were laden with trays of hot dogs, buns, mustard, and ketchup. Adrianne and Dana carried bags of marshmallows and paper goods. Sean brought the sticks, and behind him, Dylan and Rachel staggered up hauling a cooler between them.

"A feast!" Melanie said as she dropped down on the blanket beside Christina. Her cousin was waving to Dylan who waved back, but then turned away to help Rachel pass out sodas.

Christina blew out her breath. "So much for romance."

"Hey." Melanie nudged her in the side. "The evening's just starting. Besides, gooey, half-burnt marshmallows are much yummier than any guy."

"Is this seat occupied?" Sean asked as he came over, the sticks poking every which way.

"You can sit here, but watch where you're waving those sticks," Melanie said. "I don't want to lose an eye."

Sean crouched and set the bundle on the ground. Then he carefully pulled out a stick. "I fixed this just for you," he told Melanie, handing her a long skinny one with a forked end. "So you could roast three marshmallows at a time."

"All right!"

"And here's one for you, Christina." He handed her a stick with two prongs on the end. "So you and Dylan can roast yours together." He wiggled his brows like Groucho Marx. Melanie laughed, glad to see Sean acting like his old self again.

"I don't know if I'll ever get him away from Rachel," Christina said. As if on cue, Dylan came over carrying four sodas. "Anyone thirsty?"

Christina scooted close to Melanie, leaving a spot for Dylan to sit down. "I'd love one," she said.

Sean sat on the other side of Melanie just as Miss Perkins came around with the hot dogs.

"Not in the flames," she instructed in her no-nonsense voice. "Unless you like them black. The coals will roast them brown and plump."

Half an hour later, Melanie had eaten two hot dogs and was starting on her seventh marshmallow. Her lips were sticky, she had ketchup on her T-shirt, and her cheeks were flaming-hot from being so close to the fire.

"What a great night!" she told Christina as she pulled the gooey marshmallow off her stick and popped it in her mouth.

"Umm . . . and you know what would be the perfect ending?" Christina asked. "Ghost stories."

"I've got one!" Sean volunteered. Jumping up, he faced the campers, his back to the fire. "This is called the 'Tale of the Ghost Rider.'"

"Uh oh. I hope it doesn't have anything to do with Frieda trotting Felicity to death," Melanie mumbled to Christina, her mouth full of marshmallow. "I don't think Ms. Bruder would appreciate that one too much."

Sean cleared his throat, getting everybody's attention. Then, in a low voice, he began "One evening, when I was out riding, I heard someone crying. At first I thought it was just the wind moaning in the treetops, but when Jester stopped and pricked his ears, I knew it wasn't just the creaking branches."

"I rode closer to the sound, coming upon a girl sitting on a log under a huge oak tree," he continued, prowling around the fire as he addressed the circle of campers, the flickering flames throwing shadows on his face. Melanie shivered and wrapped her arms around her knees.

"Her head was buried in her hands as she sobbed pitifully. 'What's wrong?' I asked her. 'My horse threw me, and then ran off,' she replied.

"I reached my hand down. 'Climb up behind the saddle and I'll take you home.' When she stood up, I noticed she wore old-fashioned jodhpurs—the kind with the baggy legs. She took my hand, stuck her foot in

81

the stirrup, and mounted. She was so light, I don't even think Jester knew she'd gotten on.

"She told me where she lived. Then she was silent. As we trotted through the woods, I could feel her arms around my waist as she held on.

"But when I reached her house and turned to help her dismount, there was no one behind me! Where had she gone? Mystified, I got off and knocked on the door. An older woman answered. 'I'm sorry to bother you, but your daughter was thrown off her horse,' I told the woman, whose eyes grew wide. 'I brought her home, but she must have jumped off before we got here.'"

"The woman continued to stare at me in shock. 'My daughter!' she exclaimed. 'It couldn't be. My daughter fell off her horse thirty years ago and was killed instantly. You must be mistaken!'"

Melanie caught her breath, mesmerized by Sean's story. She could see why he'd gotten the lead in his school play.

"I told her I was sorry and said good-bye," Sean continued, his brows furrowed. "Mounting Jester, I rode home. I couldn't figure out what was going on. I knew I had seen a girl, and yet how could I have?"

"I finally decided it was just my imagination when we reached the woods *and* . . . " pausing, he placed his hands on his chest as if to still his beating heart, ". . . Jester stopped, stared in the direction of the big tree, and once again, I heard crying."

A mournful wail suddenly rose up from the other

82

side of the fire. Melanie jumped. All around her, kids let out shrieks.

Sean screamed dramatically. "It's her!" He pointed toward the woods. "The ghost rider!"

A shadowy figure, its arms upraised, walked stiffly toward the fire. Long hair flowed from under a riding helmet.

Instantly, Melanie recognized who it was. There was only one person that tall. "Nathan! Is that you?" she called.

"No, it's the ghost rider, you meathead," Nathan replied, stepping into the light of the fire. Jumping up, Adrianne ran over and pulled off his helmet. A wig came off with it.

"You guys," she fumed, then kissed Nathan on the cheek. He blushed so red, that everybody started laughing.

Miss Perkins clapped her hands. "That's enough of the scary stuff. How about some music?" She looked over at Sean.

"I left my guitar at the big house," he said, standing. "But I'll go get it."

"I'll go with you," Nathan said. "I want to put this stuff away." He held up the helmet and wig.

Dylan jumped up. "And I'll get my boom box in case Sean's music is as bad as his ghost story."

"Well, that was fun," Christina said when the three boys left.

Leaning back on her hands, Melanie stretched out her legs. "Yeah. And it proves I'm not the only one who can tell a ghost story or pull a prank."

Christina picked up her stick and stuck on another marshmallow. "Really. For a second there, my heart was racing."

"That's just because you were sitting next to *Dylan*," Melanie joked.

Christina threw a marshmallow at her. Melanie promptly ate it. By the time the guys came back, she was so stuffed, she never wanted to open her mouth again. But then Sean began playing some of her favorite Beatles songs, and she joined in.

It was nearly ten when Miss Perkins announced that it was time for bed. Gus hosed down the campfire, turning it into a soggy mess. Melanie helped pick up trash and followed Christina, Eliza, and Jennifer back to the kennels.

She could barely keep her eyes open. "I'm going to sleep for a week."

"Thank goodness tomorrow's Sunday," Eliza said, yawning. "There's only a trail ride scheduled for the afternoon so we can sleep in."

"Oh, really? Then who's going to feed the horses?" Christina asked.

"The horses!" The four girls groaned in unison as they staggered into their dorm room. Melanie reached into her trunk to get her towel and toiletries bag. She opened the bag and hunted for her toothbrush. She was too tired to worry about washing her face.

When she found it, she pulled it out. Brown, greasy stuff clung to the bristles. "What's this?"

"Yuck! Someone's put sticky stuff all over my comb!" Jennifer said almost at the same time.

"Oh no." Christina looked in her own bag and grimaced. With two fingers, she pulled out her hairbrush. It was covered with brown gunk. And someone had smeared a streak on the end of Jennifer's towel.

"We've been slimed," Melanie said grimly. "With peanut butter."

"But who—?" Christina started to ask, then Jennifer pointed to the back window, and exclaimed, "Look!"

"Gotcha!" had been written across one pane with lipstick. Underneath, the capital letters N, D, and S were scrawled in cursive writing.

"Nathan, Dylan, and Sean," Christina said. "No wonder they all left the campfire at the same time. Those creeps."

"But why us?" Eliza asked. Then narrowing her eyes, she glanced sharply at Melanie. "Unless they're getting back at someone who lives in this room."

Melanie forced a smile. If Nathan, Dylan, and Sean had been behind the sliming, it could only mean one thing—Sean had told the other two about her plans to raid the carriage house. Soon, it would be all over camp, and from now on, she'd definitely be accused of every prank anyone played.

Even so, she met her roommates stares with her most innocent expression. "Who could they possibly be getting back at?"

Without hesitation, all three girls pointed their fingers at her and hollered, "You!"

8

"PICNIC BY THE RIVER, PASS IT ON," RACHEL WHISPERED TO Melanie at breakfast. It was Wednesday morning. The final week of camp was half over. The instructors had worked all the campers hard on Monday and Tuesday, trying to prepare them for the weekend competition. Melanie thought a picnic sounded heavenly.

Turning to Christina who sat on her other side, Melanie said, "Picnic by the river, pass it on."

"A picnic? When?" Christina asked.

"I don't know. Ask Rachel. She's the one spreading rumors."

Christina leaned forward and peered around Melanie. "What picnic? And when?"

"I heard Perky and Frieda talking before breakfast." Rachel leaned in front of Melanie, too. "They said since it was so hot, we could have lunch by the river and swim."

"Cool."

"Hey, do you guys mind not flopping your hair in my cereal?" Melanie asked. "It's bad enough that everything we eat is sprinkled with horse hair."

"Sorry." Rachel flipped her long ponytail behind one shoulder, sending several strands of hair floating into Melanie's milk. Wrinkling her nose, Melanie pushed the bowl away.

Suddenly, Christina nudged Melanie in the ribs. Nathan was coming into the kitchen. When he spotted the two girls, he grinned and pretended to brush his teeth.

"What was that all about?" Rachel asked when he went into the other dining room.

"Oh, nothing," Melanie fibbed.

"Nathan, Dylan, and Sean smeared peanut butter all over their stuff Saturday night during the campfire," Anita said from the other side of the table.

"How'd you know?" Melanie asked.

Anita shrugged. "I thought everybody knew. Poe said that last week Sean caught you up in their rooms trying to steal their toilet paper or something."

Melanie rolled her eyes. Oh, great, just like she thought, the story had spread all over camp. She wondered why it had taken so long. Abruptly, she stood up. "Well, I guess it's time to tack up. Wouldn't want to miss a second of Frieda's sitting trots."

"Right." Christina stood up, too. When they left, Rachel was still staring curiously at them.

"What big mouths those boys have," Christina grumbled. "Now everybody knows."

"What are you worried about?" Melanie said. "Didn't you notice that no one mentioned *your* name." She tapped on her chest. "I'm the one getting all the blame."

"Sorry. But it *was* your idea to raid the boys' room in the first place."

"And it was a good idea, too. We just got caught."

The two girls hurried to A barn. When they reached the end row of stalls, Melanie checked Tuesday's points tacked on the post. Yesterday, she'd worked really hard to do everything right. Still, when she skimmed the list, she saw that Dana had only given her five points out of a total of eight. No one else in A barn had less than six points.

Melanie felt a rush of anger. It didn't seem fair. No matter how hard she tried, Dana hadn't cut her a break.

"Melanie! Telephone!"

The shout came from the house. Melanie turned to see who was calling. Miss Perkins stood on the porch, waving.

Dad! Breaking into a jog, Melanie tore across the green and up to the house. Without taking off her boots, she clomped into the office.

"Dad?" she gasped breathlessly when she picked up the receiver.

"Mel! It's so good to hear your voice."

"Where are you calling from?"

"I'm in San Francisco on business."

"California?" Almost three thousand miles away. Did that mean he wasn't going to be back in time for Saturday's competition?

"I was planning on finishing up and flying to Lexington on Friday, but— "

The instant Melanie heard the "but," tears welled in her eyes.

"—but it may not work out that way."

Melanie swallowed hard. There was such a thick lump in her throat, she couldn't say anything.

"Are you still there, honey?"

"Yes," she managed to choke out.

"I'm going to try to make it. But if I can't see you this weekend, then next. I'll bring Susan. She wants to see you."

Melanie wiped her cheeks. After clearing her throat, she inhaled shakily. She didn't want her dad to know she was crying. "That sounds great, Dad. And don't worry if you can't make it. Camp's lots of fun."

"That's great. I miss you, sweetie."

"I miss you." *More than you can imagine.*

"I'll call you Friday morning to let you know if I'll make it. I really do want to come."

And I really want you to come.

"Bye, honey."

"Bye, Dad." Slowly, Melanie set the receiver on the hook. Her heart felt like it weighed a ton. The disappointment was almost overwhelming. Brushing away her tears, she was determined not to let it get to her.

She hurried from the office. She needed to get back to the barn and tack up Trib. She couldn't afford to lose any more points. She'd promised her team.

When she reached the barn, Christina and Jennifer were already leading their horses across the green.

"I saddled Trib for you," Christina said. "Was that your dad?"

"Yes. Would you explain to Ms. Bruder that I had a phone call and that I'll be right there?"

"Sure."

Melanie jogged down the aisle, grabbing the bridle from the hook before going into the stall. When Trib pinned his ears, she ignored him.

"No time for pony tantrums," she said as she looped the reins over his neck. Quickly, she bridled him. She was buckling the throatlatch when a tidal wave of sadness swept over her.

He wasn't going to come. She just knew it.

Melanie's lower lip trembled. *Stop it! Don't cry!* she told herself. But it was no use. Throwing her arms around Trib's neck, Melanie buried her face in his fuzzy mane and sobbed.

"Do you have all your stuff?" Christina asked Melanie later that afternoon. The two were leaving the kennels, their packs stuffed with towels, sunscreen, sodas, magazines, and bagged lunches.

"I think," Melanie tried to sound enthusiastic. Swimming in the river would be fun but somehow her heart wasn't in it.

They met Anita and Poe coming out of their room.

"I heard Nathan's taking us to a spot where there's a rope swing," Anita said as the foursome headed for the parking lot.

"Do you think there are snakes?" Poe asked.

"Only anacondas," Melanie replied, straight-faced.

Poe bit her lip worriedly. "Aren't those the really long ones?"

"I thought Gus was driving us," Christina said, scanning the parking lot.

Anita shook her head. "We're walking."

Melanie glanced down at her feet. All she'd worn was the flip-flops she used to go to the shower. "If I'd known that, I would have worn my sneakers."

"It's pasture most of the way," Poe assured her.

"Too late now, anyway," Christina said when they crossed the lot and headed around the barn. "It looks as if everybody's ready to go."

A group had assembled in front of the hay-and-grain shed. Nathan had a whistle around his neck like a lifeguard. Everybody was dressed in bathing suits and T-shirts. Sean and Dylan wore baseball caps. When Melanie and Christina joined them, Rachel was already hovering around Dylan.

"Ready to fight the rapids?" Dylan asked.

"And wrestle the anacondas," Christina replied.

"I'm going to call names to see who's here," Adrianne said, pulling a piece of paper from her pocket. "Now pick a swimming buddy," she instructed when she'd finished roll call. "Then stay with that person. We don't want to lose anybody in the water."

Melanie looked over at Christina but she and Dylan were smiling goofily at each other so she knew they were partners. Anita linked arms with Poe; Rachel teamed with Bekka. Jennifer and Eliza were waving to each other.

Last one to be picked, Melanie thought gloomily.

"Mel? You want to hang with me?" Sean asked, looking a little lost himself.

Melanie gave him a big grin. "Only if you promise not to let me drown."

The walk through the pasture was long and hot, but the thought of cool water kept everybody moving. When they reached the river, sweat was rolling down Melanie's forehead.

"Last one in is a rotten egg!" she shouted as she tore off her T-shirt.

"Not until I've told everybody the rules," Adrianne hollered above her.

Sean made a disgusted noise in his throat. "Rules. How could we forget?"

Nathan and Adrianne went through the *do*s and *don't*s. Then with war whoops and screams, everybody plunged in.

The water was cool and surprisingly clear. Adrianne had warned them to stay near the rocks, which formed a sheltered cove, since the current grew swifter toward the middle of the river. Melanie was a good swimmer, so she wasn't worried. Still, she stuck close to Sean.

"Ready for the rope?" she asked him.

It hung from a high branch of a towering oak. So far, no one had wanted to take the first plunge. And no wonder. It was a ten-foot drop into the river.

Sean looked up, squinting his eyes against the sun. "You first."

The two climbed the rocks until they were under the limb. Reaching out, Melanie grasped the rope and pulled it toward her. When she peered over the edge, her heart skipped a beat. It was a lo-o-ong way down. Still, she knew she had to do it. She had to prove to everybody that she wasn't just the stupidest rider with the lowest number of points.

"Watch out for that anaconda, Mel!" Anita called.

Everybody looked up and watched her. Some of the kids were sunning on the rocks, others treaded water. Christina was floating on a rubber raft, smiling and waving at her.

Melanie gave her cousin the thumbs-up sign. Then she took three giant steps backward, grasped the rope with both hands, and ran forward.

"Eiiii!" she screamed as she sailed into the air.

"Let go!" Sean yelled.

Melanie released her grip. Shutting her eyes, she dropped into the river, the water closing over her head like a cold blanket. Immediately, she stroked and kicked, trying to head for the surface. She opened her eyes but the water was dark and murky. *Which way was up?*

For a second, she felt disoriented and panic made her

freeze. Then she remembered what she'd learned in a swimming class. Don't fight the water. Letting her body go limp, she felt herself drift upwards. As soon as she realized which way was up, she kicked with all her might.

Breaking the surface, she greedily gulped the air. On top of the rock, Sean was staring down at her with the rope in his hand. "Awesome!" she shouted.

A cheer went up, then several kids climbed up to the tree, eager to try it. Melanie swam lazily over to Christina. Hanging onto the edge of the raft, she shook her head, spraying her cousin.

"Your turn."

"Not me. Mounting Sterling's about as high as I climb."

"You don't know what you're missing." Melanie pushed away. With a Tarzan yell, Sean swung out over the water. His arms and legs flailed the air as he fell.

"I've got to do that again!" he announced when he came up, spitting and sputtering.

Melanie swam around lazily for a few more minutes, then climbed onto the rocks and lay back on her towel. The sun felt great—like a big, warm hug. And somehow, plunging in the water had helped, too. Maybe it knocked all the sad thoughts right out of her.

She was drifting off to sleep when a sharp voice made her snap awake.

"She's not going to get any better because she doesn't even care."

Melanie opened one eye, wondering who was saying what about who. Eliza and Jennifer were sitting two rocks over, their backs to Melanie. Jennifer was turned toward Eliza, and Melanie could see her mouth open and shut as if she were a handpuppet.

"I know. I can't believe she was late for this morning's lesson," Eliza said, her words muffled.

"So we might as well face facts," Jennifer's voice rose. "As long as she's on our team, we're not going to win."

With a sinking heart, Melanie turned onto her side. She knew exactly who they were talking about. *Her.*

9

SHE *HAD* BEEN LATE FOR THIS MORNING'S LESSON. BUT IT wasn't because she didn't care. She'd been crying too hard.

Drops of cold water hit Melanie's shoulder and a shadow fell over her face.

"Go away," she muttered. Not that she wanted to be alone with her gloomy thoughts

"We're supposed to stick with each other, remember?" Sean said. With exaggerated movements, he flapped his towel in the air, fanning Melanie's chilled skin before laying it down on the rock.

"Would you get settled?" Melanie grumbled, rolling onto her back.

He stuck a soda can in her face. "Thirsty?"

"Yes!" When she grabbed for it, he pulled it out of reach.

"Say ple-e-ase."

"Ple-e-ase may I have it—before I kill you!" Bolting upright, Melanie snatched it out of his hand. Christina and Dylan came over with their lunch bags and sodas. Christina had her towel wrapped around her waist. Her hair had been slicked back.

"May we join you?" she asked as she plopped onto Melanie's towel.

Melanie scooted over to give her more room. At least Christina was still her friend. Should she tell her what she'd overheard? That her teammates hated her?

No. That would be asking her cousin to choose sides. Melanie just wished she could make Eliza and Jennifer understand that she really was trying.

"So what's for lunch?" Sean asked as he opened his bag.

"I only know that Dana and Adrianne were in charge of making it," Christina said.

Gingerly, Melanie picked up her own bag. "Uh oh. If Dana made my lunch, there's probably a black widow spider in it."

"Don't kill it. It might be Dana's mother," Sean said.

"Really. I'm sure glad I'm in B barn," Dylan said. "Dana thinks she's the commandant of A barn. If you don't do everything her way, you're doomed."

Cautiously, Melanie opened her bag and peered inside. Nothing wiggly or slithery crawled out.

"I wonder what makes her so mean," Christina said.

"Adrianne told me that Dana's parents separated

this summer," Dylan said. "I met them last year when they came to the end of camp competition. I guess it's got her pretty upset."

"So she takes it out on us?" Melanie said.

"Right."

The four kids grew silent as they munched on their sandwiches. Melanie thought about what Dylan had said about Dana. It helped to explain why Dana seemed to have such a chip on her shoulder. Though it didn't explain why she had it in for Melanie.

Unless I deserve it.

The answer hit her like a pie in the face. Now that she thought about it, Melanie realized she was just like Dana. She'd let her problems with her dad interfere with her performance at camp.

Jennifer and Eliza were right. She hadn't been trying her hardest. She'd let her teammates down.

She glanced over at the two girls who were sitting with Nathan and Adrianne. She could hear snatches of their conversation. They were discussing pirouettes, flying changes, and serpentines at the canter—stuff Melanie had only read about. Not only were Eliza and Jennifer better riders than she, they knew twice as much. No wonder they thought she wasn't pulling her weight.

Should she apologize to them? And if she did, what could she say that didn't sound stupid or whiny?

"A melted candy bar!" Sean exclaimed so loudly that Melanie turned her attention back to the others.

"Just what I always wanted for dessert." He held up a Milky Way. When he pressed on the wrapper, she could see how soft it was.

"Oh, yummy." Melanie giggled. Reaching over, she squished the candy bar between her fingers. Chocolate shot out of both ends of the wrapper, plopping on Sean's lap.

"Hey!" he protested. Sticking a finger in it, he lunged at Melanie, but she had already leaped to her feet. "You'll never catch me!" Holding her nose, she jumped from the rock into the river.

When she came to the surface, Dylan and Christina were laughing. She glanced at Eliza and Jennifer. Jennifer was rolling her eyes as if she couldn't believe how immature Melanie was being. Eliza was still talking to Nathan.

I *do* need to apologize and I *do* need to try harder, Melanie decided as she kicked away from the rock. Not only for her team, but for herself.

"We're jumping eight obstacles," Nathan said, looking at the campers from his perch on the top board of the fence of the jumping arena. "You all got a chance to walk the course this afternoon. Does anyone remember the order of jumps?"

Melanie raised her hand. She and Trib were standing with the other horses and riders in her lesson group outside the ring. After the picnic, the girls had helped set up the brightly colored fences in a new arrangement for the evening lesson. Each obstacle was numbered and had a red and a white flag.

"It's a figure eight," Poe said before Nathan could call on someone, then she began reciting the sequence in which they were going to jump them.

Melanie listened carefully. So far today, Dana hadn't found one thing to fault her on. She didn't want to mess up tonight.

Nathan nodded. "Good. Now who can tell me some of the reasons you might be eliminated?"

Melanie popped her arm up. "Because you showed an obstacle to a horse before starting or after a refusal. Because you took more than sixty seconds to jump an obstacle . . ." She recited three more rules before Nathan smiled and told her to give someone else a chance.

Melanie smiled to herself. She knew them all. Eliza had warned them that Nathan would ask about eliminations and she'd been prepared.

"Anita, I'd like you to go first," Nathan said. "The jumps are set at two feet for Mushroom. I'm going to raise them for the others."

Melanie grinned excitedly. That meant Nathan was going to let her jump higher. She felt good that at least he had confidence in her.

"When you enter the arena, I'll blow my whistle to signal start time." Nathan held up the whistle dangling around his neck. "If I blow it during your round, that means to stop. During this weekend's competition a bell will be used."

"How long do we have after you blow the whistle to cross the starting line?" Poe asked.

"Sixty seconds," Melanie said quickly. "And don't forget—if you start before Nathan signals, you're eliminated."

"So many rules," Bekka complained. "How are we supposed to remember them all?"

"That's why we're practicing this evening," Nathan said. "Anita are you ready?"

Anita nodded. Mushroom had been contentedly snoozing so she had to nudge him hard with her heels to wake him up.

While Anita did her warm-up circle, Melanie went over the sequence of jumps in her head. *Gate first, brush second—*

By the time she focused back on Anita, Mushroom was cantering toward the first line of jumps.

"You'll need six strides between them!" Nathan called. Turning to Christina and Poe who had horses, he said, "You girls will ride it in five strides."

"What about me?" Melanie asked.

Nathan chuckled. "Trib's such a natural jumper, you just need to steer, hang on, and let him figure it out."

Melanie didn't think that was a compliment. Obviously, she'd been wrong. It sounded as if Nathan didn't have confidence in her. He had confidence in Trib.

After the first line, Mushroom swung wide and took the center fence, a small triangular-shaped coop. The little buckskin pony leaped it neatly, with his front legs tucked under his belly. Anita's team was doing well, Melanie remembered. And if Anita had a great performance on Saturday, her team could be the big winners.

The riders clapped heartily when Anita pulled Mushroom to a walk.

"Nice job," Nathan praised. "Melanie, you and Trib are next." He jumped off the post, landing in the soft footing of the arena. "I'm going to raise everything to two-foot six."

While he went around the ring, changing the fences, Melanie walked Trib back and forth in front of the ingate. All the rules she'd learned kept repeating in her head like a chant.

By the time Nathan gestured for her to come into the arena, Melanie's palms were perspiring. More than anything she wanted to do a good job. But what if she forgot the course? What if Trib refused a jump? What if he balked and it took more than sixty seconds to cross the starting line?

"Don't look so grim," Nathan said when she trotted past him. "Relax and let Trib do his own thing."

There was that advice again, Melanie thought. As if she couldn't ride a horse around a course. She thought back to the comment Dana had made—that she was the worst rider at camp. Well, she wasn't, and she'd just have to prove she wasn't some baby beginner.

Nathan blew the whistle. Melanie turned Trib, trotted him between the starting poles, and squeezed him into a canter. When she pointed him toward the gate, his ears pricked in anticipation and he quickened his pace.

"Oh, no you don't," Melanie muttered. "I'm the boss today." Sitting deep, she pulled him down to a slower pace. Suddenly, the fence loomed right in front of them, Trib took a choppy stride and hopped it awkwardly.

Melanie tightened up on him. Using her seat, she pushed him toward the brush. He reached it in five strides, and it was too late when Melanie realized he needed six. He leaped from so far back that Melanie had to grab mane to keep from getting left behind.

The whistle shrilled.

Startled, Melanie swung her head to see why Nathan was blowing. She hadn't gone off course. Trib hadn't refused. *What did he want?*

She circled Trib toward the instructor. When she slowed to a walk she saw the exasperated look on his face.

"What are you doing?" he demanded.

"Jumping the course."

"No, I mean what are you doing to Trib?"

"Uh, um, I'm riding him. You know, being the boss."

"Melanie, if you want to be a boss, get a manager's job in a fast-food restaurant."

Melanie flushed. "I don't understand."

"No, I can see you don't." Nathan's expression relaxed a little. Stepping closer, he put his hand on Trib's mane. "Let me explain. Every event rider wants a horse that is responsive to his or her aids, yet smart enough to figure out how to negotiate jumps on its own as well. Every *horse* wants a rider who's sensitive enough to adapt and respond to its way of going because every horse is totally different. Does that make sense?"

Melanie nodded.

"Trib is a keen, experienced pony who knows exactly how to jump a course with a little assistance from you, his rider. Instead of fighting him, be his partner. That means knowing when to let him do the job."

"Right." Melanie bit her lip. She thought she understood what Nathan was trying to say.

He smiled, softening his words. "Sometimes he's a stubborn brat and you *do* have to be the boss with him, Melanie. But you know when those times are. Now start over again."

"Okay." As she steered Trib toward the outside rail, Melanie took a deep breath. She wanted to whack herself on the helmet. How could she have completely misread Nathan's earlier advice? He hadn't been telling her she was a beginner. He was asking her to trust her horse.

Don't fight him. Be Trib's partner. And remember, you don't have to prove anything to anybody except yourself.

This time, when she cantered Trib to the gate, she let

her entire body relax. Her fingers were light on the reins, her seat swayed gently in the saddle, her legs were supportive instead of clamped.

Trib sailed over the gate, then jumped the brush in six perfect strides. Turning her head, Melanie focused on the coop. Automatically, Trib circled toward it, his canter smooth, his takeoff just right. Melanie felt lighter than air and in perfect sync with Trib as they soared over the jump, landed, angled into the corner, then headed for the outside line.

Minutes later, when they'd finished the course, Christina, Poe, Anita, and Bekka burst into cheers and applause.

Cheeks flushed, Melanie slowed Trib to a walk. Nathan gave her the thumbs up sign. "That was a blue-ribbon round. No need to do it again. Cool him off and put him away."

"Thanks." Leaning over, Melanie gave Trib a big pat on the neck. Letting her reins drop onto his neck, she walked him from the arena. Christina came jogging over on Sterling.

"That was super! One of the best courses I've seen Trib do in a long time," Christina praised. Even Poe, Bekka, and Anita were looking at her with admiration.

"Maybe I'm not the best rider on our team," Melanie told Christina. "But I'm going to work hard to become the best rider for Trib."

"Sounds good to me!" Christina agreed.

Maybe her team wouldn't lose after all.

10

MELANIE JUMPED OFF TRIB AND PULLED THE REINS OVER HIS head. She snuck a look at Nathan and when he turned his back to her, she pulled a piece of carrot from her pocket. Trib plucked it from her palm and chewed greedily.

Christina tsked. "Don't let Nathan see you feeding him a treat with his bridle on."

"Trib deserved it." She patted his neck. It was soaked with sweat. "I'm going to walk him back to the barn. When are you jumping?"

"Nathan wants me to go last. He's going to put several of the fences up to three feet." Christina smiled with excitement.

"Great! If I get Trib bathed in time, we'll come back and watch."

After running up her stirrups, she loosened the

pony's girth a notch, and then started for the barn. Trib strode ahead, tugging on the reins. "Don't step on my toes," she warned as he pulled her across the drive.

The second lesson group was working on dressage. Melanie could see several horses and riders in the warm-up field circling Jody. The rest stood outside the dressage arena with Frieda, watching Sean and Jester. Frieda was booming out suggestions so loudly that Melanie could hear her as she led Trib down the hill.

"Sean, you're working toward self-carriage. Don't try and power that horse into an extended trot . . ."

Melanie shook her head. She had to remind herself that she wasn't the only one who got criticized.

When she reached the barn, she untacked Trib. Her bridle was slick with dirty sweat. Instead of watching the video scheduled for later, Melanie knew she better clean it.

She stuck Trib in his stall and went to get warm water to bathe him. Since he'd need a lot of cooling off she could walk him back up the hill to watch Christina. She just needed to hurry.

She filled the bucket and relaxed for a minute. The evening air was warm and the barn area was quiet. Above her, barn swallows swooped and dove, catching flies. There were several nests in the eaves with fluffy babies in them. Soon, they'd be joining their parents in flight.

Trib nickered from his stall.

"I'm coming," Melanie said as she turned off the spigot, though she knew he was bellowing for one of his equine buddies. She snapped the lead to his halter and led him from his stall over to the bucket. He rubbed his face on her shoulder. "Itchy, huh?" She dipped the sponge in the bucket, wrung it almost dry, and scrubbed his face. She sloshed water on his back, concentrating on his saddlemark. Then she whisked off the water with the sweat scraper.

"Oh, you look so clean and handsome. Let's go see your girlfriend, Sterling." They went back up the hill, but when they reached the arena, Trib put down his head to graze and never looked up.

Melanie leaned her elbows on the top board of the ring. Christina was just entering the in-gate. Nathan had put a pole over the coop and raised the two fences on the outside line. Melanie knew that three feet wasn't considered high for a horse. Still they looked gigantic to her.

Sterling almost walked over them.

"That was a pretty uneven round," Bekka said when the duo finished.

"And what about all those hesitations and huge leaps?" Anita added.

Melanie frowned, annoyed at the two girls. "Sterling's really green," she reminded them. "Not like your two ponies."

"Well, excuse us for having an opinion," Anita said haughtily.

Nathan gestured for Christina to come over to him. They talked for a few minutes, then Christina did the course again. This time Sterling was smoother and more consistent.

"See?" Melanie said. "Sterling's just inexperienced. By Saturday, she's going to have the winning round. So don't count on a trophy yet, ladies." With a cocky smile, Melanie pulled Trib's head up and went to meet her cousin.

"Nice job!" she complimented. Christina was smiling from ear to ear.

"The first round was pretty sticky," Christina said. "I'm glad Nathan made us go again."

"You know, Eliza and Jennifer are all hyper about winning the team trophy this weekend," Melanie said as Christina dismounted and ran up her stirrups. "I think we've got a chance. Especially with rounds like we both had this evening."

"We might." Lifting up the saddle flap, Christina loosened her girth.

Anita, Poe, and Bekka rode past. "Nice job," Poe told Christina, in a begrudging tone. Anita and Bekka didn't even look their way.

"What's wrong with them?" Christina asked.

"They're jealous. Plus, I sort of put them in their places. They think their teams are going to win. Well, I told them *we* are winning that trophy."

Christina shook her head in disbelief. "Mel, you sure do know how to make people mad at you."

"I know." Melanie dropped her chin, pretending to look chastised. "I just can't help it."

Christina giggled. They led the horses back to the barn. The dressage lessons must have been over, too, since the arena and warm-up field were empty.

When they reached A barn, Christina untacked Sterling. Melanie put Trib away, opened her trunk, and started gathering her tack-cleaning supplies.

Eliza led Flash down the aisle. The big black Thoroughbred wore a new blue-and-white cooler draped over his back. "He looks gorgeous," Melanie said. She was dying to tell Eliza how well she had done this evening.

"He is the handsomest guy," Eliza cooed as she kissed him on the nose.

"How was the dressage lesson?"

"Super. Frieda's a whip-cracker, but she really teaches you a lot. She helped me get Flash to do a perfect leg-yield to shoulder-in, something he's always had trouble with."

"Maybe we'll have a chance at that team trophy after all." When Eliza didn't say anything, Melanie pulled her saddle soap from the trunk.

Apologize to her, Melanie told herself. Only it wasn't that easy.

Angry voices made Melanie look up. Several kids were in the aisle of B barn, talking loudly. Christina stuck her head out of Sterling's stall. "What's going on?"

"Maybe Rachel broke a fingernail," Melanie joked.

"Sounds more serious than that," Eliza said, putting Flash in his stall.

Melanie stood up just as Poe and two older campers named Sara and Julie marched across the green, angry expressions on their faces. Melanie didn't know the older girls that well because they kept their horses in B barn and had lessons with the other group, but she knew they were on Poe's team.

The three stopped in front of Melanie. Plopping her hands on her hips, Poe declared, "We don't think it's funny."

"What? My crack about Rachel's fingernails?" Melanie had no idea what they were talking about.

"No. The red and white confetti you threw in our stalls. We're going to have to completely clean them out and replace the sawdust."

Melanie's eyes widened in astonishment. "Confetti?"

Behind her, Melanie heard a stall door open and Christina came up to stand beside her. "Why are you accusing Melanie?" she asked. "Anybody could have done it."

"Only she was the one bragging that her team was going to win. We figured she was celebrating early," Poe said, her braces flashing. "Besides, she was the only one down here alone. Remember? Nathan sent her back early."

Melanie opened her mouth but nothing came out.

"Well, it wasn't Melanie," Christina stated firmly.

"And I know it *was* Melanie," Poe said. "She's the only one with a bad attitude. She's the only one who will do *anything* to win."

"We've already reported this to Miss Perkins," Sara said, and after shooting Melanie an ugly look, the three stomped away.

Christina gave Melanie an awkward pat on the shoulder. "Ignore them," she said.

"How can I?" Melanie stood glued to the aisle floor. "Did you hear them? Not only do they think I'm horrible, but they've reported it to Miss Perkins."

Eliza turned and went back into Flash's stall without saying a word.

"It's not like confetti's going to hurt anything," Christina added.

"It's not the confetti," Melanie said, a sob rising in her throat. "It's the fact that I haven't done anything wrong and yet the whole camp's turned against me." Her voice grew thick with tears. "It's like some horrible nightmare and it's happening to me!"

Just then the bell rang at the big house.

"Miss Perkins wants us all in the common room for a meeting!" Nathan shouted down the hill.

Melanie gave Christina a horrified look. "You know what that means."

"Maybe she just wants to tell us about the event this weekend," Christina said, trying to sound encouraging. But fifteen minutes later, when the two entered the common room, Melanie could tell by the stern expres-

113

sion on Miss Perkins's face that the meeting wasn't about the competition.

Christina wound her way into the room and sat on the arm of the sofa. Feeling awkward, Melanie huddled by the door, hoping no one noticed she was there.

"It has come to my attention," Miss Perkins began after all the campers and instructors were seated, "that certain persons are playing pranks. Every summer we have friendly rivalry going on between teams; however, this session it has gotten out of hand. If I hear about any more jokes being played, and if I find out who is responsible, that person will not be allowed to compete with his or her team this weekend."

A collective gasp went around the room. Melanie's jaw dropped. The event was the highlight of the clinic. Not being allowed to compete was tough punishment.

Poe raised her hand. "What if we know who's been playing the pranks?"

"Do you have proof?" Miss Perkins asked.

"Uh, no, but it's pretty obvious," she said, casting a sideways glance at Melanie.

As if following Poe's lead, several other campers looked her way. Melanie froze against the doorjamb. Suddenly, it seemed as if every pair of eyes in the room were staring accusingly at her—Adrianne's, Bekka's, Miss Perkins's, Sean's, even Christina's.

Heat rushed into Melanie's face. *They all think I'm guilty,* she realized. *They think I should be disqualified from the competition.*

114

Melanie flew out the door and onto the porch. She leaped down the steps and raced away. She wanted to run as far away from camp as she could and never come back.

"Melanie, are you asleep?" Christina whispered two hours later. Melanie didn't move. Keeping her breathing steady, she tried to sound as if she was in a deep sleep.

It must have worked because Christina sighed. A second later, Melanie heard the creak of Christina's bunk and the thunk of her sneakers hitting the floor.

Melanie opened one eye. She could just see Eliza's glow-in-the-dark clock. It was almost nine-thirty.

After the incident in the common room, Melanie had run to the jumping arena. Hiding behind a standard, she'd cried for a few minutes. But feeling sorry for herself quickly grew boring. When she'd figured everybody was finished at the barn, she went back and cleaned her saddle and bridle. Scrubbing the reins and polishing the bit had helped her feel better. And at least tomorrow, Dana wouldn't be able to find fault with her tack.

When she was finally done, she'd gone back to her room. She passed the big house, pausing in the shadows to listen to the sound of the video. All the kids were laughing, so it must have been a funny movie. Still, there was no way she was going inside to watch.

115

She'd showered, read for a while, and thought a while. How had things gotten so messed up? How was she going to make the kids believe she wasn't guilty?

And what if she was disqualified from the competition? Her father would be so disappointed in her. He'd probably enroll her in some boarding school that had bars on the windows. She'd never get to visit Whitebrook again.

"I think you're playing possum," Christina's voice floated up from below, breaking into Melanie's gloomy thoughts. "So if you are, listen up. *I*, Christina Reese, do not believe that *you*, Melanie Graham, had anything to do with the confetti or the switched bridles or the other stuff. Do you hear me?"

Melanie nodded, but didn't say a word.

"And if you are accused, I'll stick up for you. So when you're feeling sorry for yourself, just remember that." The bed creaked again and Melanie heard the sheet being pulled up.

I'll remember. Smiling to herself, Melanie rolled over on her side. She was glad Christina was her cousin. And her friend.

Melanie plumped up her pillow, suddenly exhausted. It had been a lo-o-ong day. Closing her eyes, she promptly fell asleep.

A loud yell woke her after what seemed like just a little while later. At first Melanie thought she was dreaming, and Poe was in her face yelling, "Liar! Liar!"

Then she sat up, realizing someone was shouting, "Fire! Fire!"

"Fire?" Eliza cried out. She switched on the bedside table lamp. Jennifer sat up and blinked her eyes sleepily.

"I heard someone yelling it, too," Melanie said, panic creeping into her voice. She jumped down from the top bunk.

"What's going on?" Christina asked, squinting in the bright light.

"Someone's yelling 'fire.'" Melanie grabbed a T-shirt from the bedpost and slipped it on over her nightshirt. She was the first out the door.

Several other campers had awakened and were milling around outside the kennels half asleep.

Melanie ran swiftly across the lawn barefoot, slowing between the carriage house and the big house. There was no sign of fire in either of the buildings.

The barns! She looked down the hill. Her heart leaped into her throat.

Smoke and flames billowed from the storage shed. It was filled with hay and sawdust. Melanie knew that any second, it might burst into flames.

She raced down the hill. Trib, Sterling, Flash, and Geronimo were in the stalls closest to the shed. She had to get them out of the barn before it caught on fire, too!

11

MELANIE FLEW TOWARD A BARN. SOMEONE WAS ALREADY IN the aisle. "You get Trib and Sterling. I'll get Geronimo and Flash." It was Sean.

Melanie plucked Trib's halter from the hook on his stall door. She knew not to try and get Sterling first. The mare would be half crazy.

For once, Trib was easy to catch. As Melanie fumbled at the buckle on his halter, she could hear the crackle of flames and smell the thickening smoke. Fear made her fingers tremble, but she tried to stay calm. She knew she couldn't help much if she panicked.

As Melanie pushed open the stall door, Christina ran past with Eliza. The two girls went to get their horses. Melanie paused a second to look at the shed. Orange flames licked from the window that faced A barn. That was where the grain was kept. When the sparks spread to the other side, the hay would catch on fire and go wild.

Miss Perkins came charging across the green wearing a bathrobe. "I've called 911. The fire department should be here in about five minutes. In the meantime, put the horses from A barn in the jumping ring," she instructed, her voice rising above the confusion and noise. "Put the horses from B barn in the back pasture. We'll have to worry about kicks later."

Dashing up to Melanie, Sean thrust Geronimo's lead into her hand. "Take Jennifer's horse. I'm going to organize a bucket brigade."

By this time, the green was swarming with people. Gus had arrived from his house trailer which was located behind the tractor shed. He carried a coiled hose across his shoulder.

Melanie halted the two horses and waited for Sterling. When Christina came out of the stall, the mare was dancing excitedly. "Follow us!" Melanie called.

Melanie jogged up the hill, a horse on each side. This time, Trib didn't need urging. Eliza, Christina, and several other campers and their horses trailed in a line behind her.

She opened the gate into the jumping ring and let Trib go. He trotted to the far side. With a toss of her head, Sterling cantered after him. By the time all the horses from A barn had been turned loose, it looked like a small herd was in the ring.

"What if Flash panics or gets kicked?" Eliza asked

worriedly. "He's never been turned out with other horses."

"Better than being burned," Melanie said. "Besides, you can't stay up here and hold him. Sean needs us. He's organizing a bucket brigade."

Suddenly, Flash burst from the group of milling horses. His eyes were white-rimmed, his nostrils flared. Nickering deep in his throat, he galloped to the far end of the arena, narrowly missing standards and poles. Without slowing down, he leaped over the ring fence.

Eliza screamed. "He jumped out!"

Head high, Flash flew down the hill back toward the barn.

"He's going to try and go back in his stall!" Eliza cried.

Without hesitating, Melanie tore after him. By the time she reached the green, Flash was galloping in crazy circles around everybody. The smoky fire and the dodging campers only made him panic more.

Running into his stall was dangerous, but Melanie knew it might be the only way she'd be able to catch him. When she reached his stall, she pulled his grain tub from the wall. Then she stood outside the door and shook it while making inviting noises. She could see Jennifer on the right side of the green. She and several of the other kids had made a human barrier to keep Flash from running down the drive toward the road.

Flash careened in the open space between the barns,

scattering campers. Then abruptly, he changed direction, crossed the green, and zoomed into his stall.

Going in after him, Melanie slammed the door shut. "Easy, easy." Reaching up, she stroked his neck which glistened with sweat. Foam flecked his mouth and the muscles in his neck and shoulders quivered.

"Come on." She snapped the lead to his halter. "Let's get Eliza, then join the other horses. Wouldn't you rather be with them?"

Lowering his head, he pushed her with his nose. Cautiously, Melanie opened the door. She didn't want him to bolt again.

She led him down the aisle in the opposite direction from the fire. He was huge and scared and any minute he could rear or lash out. But Melanie wasn't afraid of him. He reminded her of Pirate, the blind ex-racehorse, who'd also needed a lot of reassurance when his eyesight started to deteriorate.

Eliza rushed up. "Is he all right?"

"Just scared to death." Melanie gave him one more pat and handed the rope to Eliza.

"Perky told me to take him up by the other horses but hold him outside the ring," Eliza said, leading him away.

"Right." Melanie got a sinking feeling in her stomach. She was the one who'd told Eliza to leave him in the ring in the first place. Eliza would probably blame her for his escape.

But she'd have to worry about that later. Now she had to help put out the fire.

Already, a short line of campers wound from the spigot to the shed. Someone had pulled buckets from the stalls. Poe was filling them at the spigot. She passed one to Rachel, who passed it to the next person until it reached Sean who threw the water on the burning shed. Then Sean handed the empty bucket to Nathan who ran it back to Poe. On the other side of the green, Gus had hooked the hose to a spigot in the tractor shed and was spraying down the roof of the hay shed.

Melanie got behind Christina who was next to Dylan. Without a word, she grabbed the next bucket and passed it on. She watched Sean throw water onto the fire. The flames sizzled, then blazed right up again.

It was going to take more than buckets of water, Melanie realized, her horror growing. They'd saved the horses, but if the barns burned, a big part of the camp would be destroyed.

"It's not slowing it down!" Christina shouted. Her face glowed in the light of the fire. Sweat trickled down her temples.

Melanie wiped her forehead on her sleeve. "I know. But we've got to keep trying."

The sudden whir of the fire engines sent a ripple of excitement through the line. When a big, red engine pulled down the drive and stopped, cheers went up.

"Let them through!" Perky ordered.

Still clasping a bucket, Melanie stepped out of the way. It only took a minute for the firefighters to stretch out their long hoses. Ten minutes later, the flames had died down. Two firefighters carrying axes strode to the shed. They chopped through the wooden wall so the hose could be directed into the interior.

Twenty minutes later it was all over.

Relieved, Melanie sagged against the wall of A barn.

"That was a close one," Christina said. She stood in front of Sterling's open stall door. Dylan and Sean were next to her. They wore T-shirts and cutoffs. Sean's face was gray with soot and he looked exhausted.

"What if the barn had caught fire?" Christina asked, a catch in her voice. "We would have lost the horses."

Melanie shuddered. "I don't even want to think about it."

The four watched as the firefighters, dressed in heavy, protective suits and helmets, moved around the shed, making sure everything was out.

"Thank goodness someone saw the fire and sounded the alarm," Dylan said. "Was that you, Sean?"

Sean nodded. "I got up to use the bathroom. When I looked out the window, I saw smoke coming from the shed."

"Wow. It's good you reacted quickly," Christina said.

"Sean!" Miss Perkins strode across the green. Her hair was in disarray and since she wasn't wearing her glasses, she squinted at each camper as she passed.

Stepping from the shadows, Sean called, "Yes."

"Mr. Braznowski, the fire chief, wants to talk to you. See if you can help reconstruct what happened. Miserable thing, this," she added with a shake of her head. "Thank goodness it didn't get out of hand."

"Does anyone know how it started?" Melanie asked.

"No. I'm sure there will be an investigation," she replied before following Sean.

"Should we check the horses?" Christina asked.

"Yes, then I want to hear what the fire chief says." Melanie made sure Trib was okay and went over to the fire truck.

"No, I didn't see anyone," Sean was telling the fire chief. "When I saw the smoke from the window, I ran outside to see what was going on. I didn't realize the shed was on fire until I was halfway across the green. I ran back to the house and called Perky, I mean Miss Perkins. Then I alerted everyone else. I knew we had to move the horses."

Mr. Braznowski nodded. "Very quick thinking. And who organized the bucket brigade?"

"Sean." Miss Perkins beamed at him. By now, Christina, Dylan, Rachel, and several other campers were clustered around listening.

"I'd read about it in a history book," Sean said. "Before they had fire-fighting equipment that was the only way people could put out a fire."

"Your actions saved not only the shed, but the barns. It's been hot and dry and the sparks probably would have ignited the other buildings." Mr. Braznowski clapped Sean on the back. "Good job, son."

"Thanks," Sean muttered, staring awkwardly at the

ground as if embarrassed. "But everybody helped. And Gus kept the rest of the shed watered down so it wouldn't catch."

"My hero," Melanie whispered to Christina.

"I'll need to talk with Gus, too," Mr. Braznowski said.

"Can you tell how the fire started?" Miss Perkins asked.

"Not unless we find evidence. My crew is checking everything out right now."

"Braz," a female fire fighter called as she pushed her way past Melanie. "We found some matches on the ground about ten feet from the shed. You better call Arson."

"Matches!" Perky's mouth dropped open. "That can't be. Smoking is strictly forbidden on the grounds."

"No one said anyone was smoking, Miss Perkins," the fire chief said gravely. "Now if you'll excuse me for a minute." He followed the fire fighter to the shed. The two examined something on the ground.

"But who would mess with matches around the shed?" Melanie whispered to Christina.

Her cousin shook her head as if bewildered, too. "Not one of the campers, that's for sure. We all know how dangerous fire is around barns."

"Miss Perkins," a deep voice drawled from outside the group. Gus pushed his way through the kids. His leathery face was streaked with black, and his eyes were bloodshot from the smoke.

"Gus," Miss Perkins touched the man's shoulder,

126

"thank you for helping save the shed. Mr. Braznoswki, the fire chief, would like to speak to you. He's hoping you might know something about the fire."

Gus nodded. "I do know something about the fire." He held up his hand. When Melanie realized what he was holding, she let out a little squeak. Christina turned to stare at her.

"I found this flip-flop behind the shed," Gus said. "My guess is the person who started the fire left it in her hurry to get away."

"Her?" Perky repeated.

"Ma'am, it's pink. It most likely belongs to a girl."

Perky took the flip-flop and held it above her head. "Does anyone know who this belongs to?" she demanded.

Melanie swallowed hard. She could lie and say she'd never seen it before in her life, but that would only make it worse.

Slowly, her heart hammering like a drum, Melanie raised her hand. "It's mine."

12

"WHAT IS *YOUR* FLIP-FLOP DOING BEHIND THE SHED?" MISS Perkins asked, her gaze bearing down on Melanie.

Melanie could only shake her head. She didn't even remember when she'd last worn them.

"I know." Christina stepped forward. "It dropped out of her pack this afternoon when we walked back from the river."

Melanie gave her cousin a startled look. Christina could be right. She had walked back barefoot.

Miss Perkins pressed her lips together. "We will find out what happened," she addressed all the campers. "And when we do, the matter will be treated with utmost seriousness."

The director turned and left the group with Gus. Melanie stood rigid, afraid to move. She could feel the stares of the instructors and campers.

This time, they weren't silently accusing her of the stupid pranks. Setting the shed on fire was deadly serious and she could get in big trouble. A lot bigger trouble than being disqualified from the competition. Still, Melanie wasn't going to run from their stares. She was innocent—no matter what they thought.

Linking her arm with Melanie's, Christina pulled her from the crowd. "Come on," she said. "Let's check on Sterling and Trib."

Melanie stumbled after her as if in a daze. Silently, the two cousins went up the hill. Melanie knew Christina was as upset as she was, but she didn't know what to say to her.

Abruptly, Christina stopped and whirled to face her. "Look, Mel, I know you didn't set that fire," she declared. Her lips trembled. "I can't believe anyone would even think you did. It's just so unfair!" Covering her face with her hands, Christina burst into tears.

Melanie patted her shoulder. "Gee, Cuz, don't cry. There's no reason you should get dragged into this, too. I'll handle it myself."

"No you won't!" Christina dropped her hands. Her eyes were filled with tears. "You won't handle this yourself. We're cousins and friends and we'll deal with it together."

Melanie felt tears well in her own eyes. "Thanks," she blubbered. For a minute, the two hugged each other.

"What is going on?" Eliza came up with Flash. Instantly, Melanie and Christina sprang apart.

"They're accusing Melanie of setting the shed on fire!" Christina blurted.

Melanie winced. She couldn't believe Christina had told Eliza. The older girl already hated her enough.

"Gus found her stupid flip-flop by the barn," Christina rushed on. "Everybody jumped to conclusions, figuring Melanie dropped it after torching the shed. Have you ever heard anything so stupid?"

Melanie wanted to stick her fingers in her ears. No way did she want to hear Eliza's answer.

"That *is* stupid," Eliza said, and Melanie did a double take.

"What did you say?" she asked.

"I said that's stupid. You wouldn't set the shed on fire."

"But, I thought—" Melanie stammered.

Eliza smoothed Flash's forelock. "Okay, so I did think you were the one who switched the bridles in B barn and threw confetti in the stalls. But pulling pranks is one thing. Endangering horses' lives is totally different. One thing I do know about you, Melanie," she said, and gave her a sincere smile, "is that you love animals. You would never do anything to hurt one."

"I agree," Christina said firmly.

Melanie's shoulders sagged with relief. "Thanks, guys. It means a lot that you believe me. Now we have to convince Perky. She's definitely on the warpath."

"I know what we need to do," Christina said. "After we check the horses, we'll go to the room and find your

131

other flip-flop. I remember you sticking them both in your pack. One had to have fallen out when we walked back from the river."

"That's a great idea, Christina. Except when we find the match in my pack, it won't prove that I'm not guilty."

"Of course it will!"

"No." Melanie let out her breath. "It will only prove that the flip-flop Gus found behind the shed really is mine."

"She's right," Eliza pointed out. "Unless someone saw it fall from the pack, there's no way to prove Melanie didn't lose it tonight."

Christina groaned. "That's crazy. Then we just need to march down there and tell Perky there's no way Melanie did it. I mean, you were in bed all night. At least you were in bed when Sean yelled fire. I saw you."

"I did, too," Eliza chimed in.

"That doesn't mean anything, either. I could have run back to the kennels and jumped in bed." Melanie started walking toward the ring. The horses had quieted down. Trib and Sterling were standing side by side, chewing on each other's necks.

"There goes Sterling's beautiful mane," Christina grumbled.

Melanie plopped her arms on the top board and rested her chin on them. "At least Trib has plenty of mane to spare."

Halting behind them, Eliza let Flash graze. "When can we put the horses back in their stalls?"

"When the firefighters leave," Christina guessed, yawning so wide her jaw cracked. "What time is it anyway?"

"Way after midnight," Eliza said. "I glanced at the clock when Sean yelled fire. It was eleven-thirty."

"Maybe Perky will let us sleep in the morning," Melanie mumbled into her arms.

"Don't count on it," Christina said. "She and Frieda will have us up bright and early doing mounted exercises."

"Where is Frieda?" Melanie asked. "She couldn't have slept through all the excitement."

"She went to Lexington overnight for some meeting of the dressage association," Eliza explained. "But I'm sure she'll rush back here when she hears what happened."

Melanie let out dismal sigh. "Oh, goodie. I can't wait."

"As you all discovered, there is no grain for morning feed," Miss Perkins announced after breakfast Thursday morning. Everybody was assembled in the common room. The director stood by the hearth in front of the fireplace, Dana, Nathan, Jody, and Adrianne flanking her like bodyguards.

Melanie was sitting as far in the back as she could. All through breakfast the topic of conversation was the fire. No one came right out and accused her, but when she'd walked into the kitchen, several kids had fallen silent. And earlier, when she was pushing the wheelbarrow across the green after mucking Trib's stall, she'd noticed the suspicious glances thrown her way.

"I'm sure your ponies won't starve to death," Perky continued. "Though they may try and convince you otherwise. Give them extra hay if necessary. Gus is picking up grain this afternoon. It will be stored in the tractor shed. Are there any questions?"

When no one said anything, she cleared her throat and went on, "An arson investigator will be snooping about today. We will ignore it. Camp will carry on as usual."

Someone's hand shot up. Melanie couldn't see who it was. "Is there any new information on how the fire started?" the person asked, and Melanie recognized Poe's voice.

"The chief determined that the fire started in a pile of feedbags. The matchbook came from the kitchen. Sloppy housekeeping on our parts. The entire camp will be inspected today for other possible fire hazards. This won't happen again."

Miss Perkins glanced down at her clipboard and began to read the lesson assignments. "As you noticed, today you are working with your team," she said when she was through. "The instructors will help you determine the strengths and weaknesses of each member in hopes that it will help you with the weekend's competition."

When Perky paused, Adrianne stepped forward. "Tomorrow, the horses will have a light workout in the morning, probably a trail ride."

Cheers went up around the room. That was the best news Melanie had heard all morning.

"Then they'll have the afternoon off." Another round of cheers started up, but Adrianne smiled gleefully. "But you won't. Tack, clothes, and horses must be spotless. Saturday you'll need to be up by six, so it all must be done by Friday night."

Groans replaced the cheers.

"Now before you leave," Miss Perkins called above the noise. "I need to say one last thing."

Uh oh. Melanie's arms prickled. She had an idea what Perky was going to say.

"We are very serious about investigating this fire. At this time *no one* is being accused. But when we do find the guilty party, we will act swiftly."

Melanie shifted uncomfortably as several kids turned to look at her. She wanted to glare defiantly at them but dropped her gaze instead. She'd alienated enough people already.

"Anyone with information about the fire should come forth as soon as possible." Miss Perkins bobbed her head once as if to emphasize her point. "Now tack up your ponies."

Melanie was the first one out the door.

"Wait up, Melanie!"

Without slowing, Melanie glanced over her shoulder. Jennifer was hurrying to catch up. Melanie wasn't sure she wanted to hear what her teammate had to say. Jennifer wasn't exactly on her side.

"What?" Melanie asked when Jennifer fell into stride beside her.

"I just wanted to tell you that I agree with Eliza and Christina," Jennifer said. "I don't think you had anything to do with the fire either."

Cocking one brow, Melanie eyed her suspiciously. "That's a switch."

"What do you mean?"

"I overheard you and Eliza talking about me at the river yesterday."

Jennifer's face turned pink. "Well, I was really mad at you."

"I can understand why." Melanie took a deep breath. *Now's the time to apologize.* "I mean, you were right about me not pulling my weight on the team. When my dad didn't show at the picnic last week, it really bummed me out and I quit trying. I'm really sorry."

"That's okay. I went a little overboard on this point thing. The fire put the whole competition in perspective. I mean, what if I had lost Geronimo? The idea made winning seem not so important."

"Oh, really?" Melanie's eyes glinted with determination. "Personally, I think we should kick butt."

Jennifer started to giggle hysterically. "Sounds good to me!" she agreed. Stopping in front of A barn, the two girls high-fived and Melanie went over to Trib's stall.

The pony had his head stuck over the bottom door. When he spotted Melanie, he nickered excitedly.

"Oh, so *now* you love me. Well, sorry, but there's no grain this morning no matter how cute you are," she teased, feeling lighter. As long as her teammates were on her side, she could handle anything. Well, *almost* anything.

Trib bobbed his head, then butted her with his nose.

"Hey! Abuse isn't going to work either." Opening her trunk, she pulled out his bridle. Dana came down the aisle with a clipboard in her hand.

"There's a speck of dust there, and a trace of gunk here," Melanie recited out loud, gesturing right and left. "And Trib pooped in his feed bucket last night. Oh, and don't forget burning down the feed shed. That's worth at least minus six points."

Dana gave her a frosty look. "Not funny, Graham."

Melanie's grin faded. She thought about what Dylan had said about Dana's parents getting a divorce. "You're right. It isn't funny, and I didn't mean to offend you. Though it sure would be nice to see you smile for once. It wouldn't kill you, you know."

For a second, Melanie thought Dana was going to snap at her. But then the junior instructor shrugged, and her gruff look softened. "No. I guess it wouldn't. But don't hold your breath," she added.

Amazed that Dana hadn't chewed her out or, worse, called her an arsonist, Melanie watched her hustle down the aisle. Maybe this apologizing and being nice stuff really worked, she thought.

Eliza came out of Flash's stall at the other end of the barn to get her saddle. Melanie looped the bridle over her shoulder and, after taking a deep breath, headed down the aisle toward her to apologize.

13

MELANIE JUMPED WHEN SHE HEARD THE DOOR SLAM. IT WAS after lunch and she was sitting on the floor of her room, polishing her high black boots. Before she could even look up, Christina had squatted beside her.

"It's Dana!" her cousin declared.

"You're Dana?" Melanie teased as she buffed the leather, trying to bring out the shine. "I thought you were Christina."

"Be serious." Christina plucked the rag from Melanie's fingers. "I mean that Dana's the one who started the fire."

"Dana?" Melanie snapped her head around. Christina was staring at her with a solemn expression.

"Yes. I should have figured it out earlier. She set it out of spite, then framed you. I bet she's the one who pulled the pranks and framed you, too."

Melanie stared at her cousin, wide-eyed. She thought back to this morning when she'd seen a glimpse of Dana's human side. "No. I can't imagine Dana doing that. Remember what you said before? Dana's bossy and picky, but she's not vindictive. Yesterday, she even gave me seven points. That's pretty decent."

"That was just to lull you into thinking she's a nice person," Christina said. Sitting back on her heels, she tapped her lip. "Now we just need to prove it. Maybe Anita or Poe saw her leave the room last night. Or maybe someone saw her swipe the matches from—"

"And maybe if pigs had wings they could fly," Melanie cut in. "I don't think it was any of the campers. We all know how dangerous fire is around barns. And who would want to risk the life of his or her horse?"

"True." Christina's shoulders drooped as if all the air had gone out of her, but then she straightened. "Still, I'm going to keep an eye on her."

Melanie took the rag back from Christina. "You do that," she said, wiping it on the can of polish cradled in her lap.

"Well, it's more than you're doing," Christina huffed. "Everybody's pointing their fingers at you and you're not even trying to prove them wrong."

Melanie bristled. "I didn't do anything so I shouldn't have to prove them wrong. You know, innocent until proven guilty?"

"Right." Christina pushed herself off the floor. "That

may work in the courts, but not at Camp Saddlebrook. If I were you, I'd work a little harder to find the bad guy—or girl." She stomped across the room, and flung open the door. "If for no other reason than we need to find the real arsonist before the person tries it again."

Melanie looked sharply at her. "Again? Wow, I never thought about that."

"Then it's about time you did," Christina said, leaving with a dramatic toss of her head.

Melanie put the boot on the floor slowly. She hadn't thought about an arsonist. She'd decided the fire was an accident. Maybe it was started by a couple of the older campers when they'd hidden behind the shed to sneak a cigarette.

But what if someone had set it on purpose?

She shook her head. No, that didn't make sense. No one at camp would risk the death of his or her horse.

Unless it was someone at camp who didn't have a horse.

That narrowed it down to four people. Melanie instantly eliminated Perky—she'd been director for a million years. And Frieda had been in Lexington. That left only two people—Mrs. Henderson and Gus.

Mrs. Henderson lived somewhere in town. Melanie couldn't imagine the elderly woman, who looked like she loved her own cooking, creeping to the barn in the middle of the night. On the other hand, Gus lived on the grounds and made no bones about disliking kids and horses.

A chill rippled up Melanie's back. *Was Gus the arsonist? And if he was, why did he do it?*

Her mind whirled, trying to remember if she'd witnessed any arguments he might have had with Frieda or Perky. She thought back to the morning Gus had been mowing. Had Perky been chewing him out? He sure acted like it. Or maybe they were threatening to fire him or dock his pay. In fact, she could think of lots of reasons he might have done it.

In fact, it was kind of a coincidence that he'd been the one to find her flip-flop. Maybe he'd even put it there.

Melanie jumped to her feet and the can of polish fell to the floor. She had to tell someone.

She was halfway out the door when she realized she couldn't tell anyone. Frieda or Perky would just think she was trying to pin the blame on somebody else. She'd have to find proof first.

But how? And where?

Christina would help. She was down at the barn evening up Sterling's mane. Melanie hoped that no one was with her.

When she reached A barn, the aisle was deserted. Christina had borrowed someone's portable radio. It was propped on a bucket, playing loudly.

"Chris!" Melanie hollered into Sterling's stall. The mare threw up her head, startled.

"Hey!" Christina sputtered. "You're going to make me mess up her mane worse than Trib already did."

"This is important. I think I figured out who did it. *Gus.*"

"Gus?" Christina repeated, her eyes still on Sterling's mane. "That's as farfetched as me accusing Dana."

"No, it isn't." Melanie told her why. When she was finished, Christina was staring at her. "You could be right. How are we going to prove it?"

"What if we found something incriminating in his trailer? Like another matchbook like the one that was found, or a letter saying he was fired."

"You mean sneak into his trailer? No way." She shook her head vehemently. "We were already caught sneaking into Sean's room. It's obviously not something we're good at."

"Only this time we'll make sure Gus isn't around. He left to get feed, remember? We just need to do it right now." Opening the door, she stepped aside and grinned pleadingly.

"All right. But I'm not going inside. I'll stand watch."

"Deal."

The two walked nonchalantly across the green and around the back corner of B barn. When they were out of sight of the kennels and the house, they dashed to the tractor shed. Melanie could see the end of Gus's trailer sticking from behind the low building.

"Piece of cake," she said to Christina, who was nervously gnawing a nail. "We'll hear Gus when he pulls his truck up to unload the grain."

"What if the trailer's locked?" Christina asked.

"It won't be," Melanie said confidently, though she had no idea if it would be or not.

When they reached the door, Melanie gestured for Christina to wait at the bottom of the metal steps. Cautiously, she turned the knob. The door swung open.

Melanie took a deep breath. She knew that what she was doing was wrong. At the same time, she had no choice. If Gus was the arsonist, he had to be stopped.

She peeked in, looking both ways. The trailer had a small kitchen to the right, a narrow living room to the left. A hall ran down the far side, probably leading to a bath and bedroom. Everything looked brand new.

"I'm only going to stand guard for five minutes!" Christina hissed behind her, then gave her a push. "So hurry up!"

Melanie stumbled inside. Quickly, she hunted through the kitchen, hoping to find a telltale pack of matches. The counters and cupboards were neat and spotless. So clean in fact, she didn't find a single crumb.

Disappointed, she walked into the living room. A big-screen TV took up one whole wall. On the other wall, a small desk was built into some shelves. Papers and mail were stacked on top in neat piles. Melanie couldn't figure out how someone who looked like such a bum could keep such a tidy house.

"Hurry up!" Christina called in a low voice.

"One more minute." Melanie flipped through the stack of mail on the desk, careful not to mess it up. A piece of paper with Camp Saddlebrook letterhead caught her eye.

This is it! she thought excitedly. The note from Perky telling Gus that he was fired!

Only when Melanie skimmed it, her excitement died. "Dear Gus", the note read. "Enclosed is a bonus for the month of July. You have been a loyal employee. Thank you for all your hard work."

She checked the date on top just in case. It was current.

"Melanie! This is a warning! Then I'm leaving."

Melanie hurried to the door. There was no reason to look further. A new trailer, a big screen TV, and a bonus—she didn't think Gus would be stupid enough to get himself fired from such a cushy job.

"Well?" Christina asked, her eyes bright with curiosity.

"Nothing."

"You mean I was standing out here frightened to death for nothing?"

"Right." As the two girls headed back to A barn, Melanie told her cousin what she had found.

Christina sighed. "Bummer."

"So if it's not Dana, and it's not Gus, then who could it be?" Melanie asked, her brow furrowed.

"Mrs. Henderson?" Christina quipped, and the two girls started laughing.

They were walking around the corner of the tractor shed when Gus drove up in the truck. Shrieking, Christina jumped a foot in the air.

"Cool it," Melanie whispered. "Or he'll know something is up."

"Something is up," Christina whispered back. "My heart rate."

Parking the truck by the shed, Gus got out. Melanie went right up to him. "Thank goodness you got the grain," she said, patting a stack of bagged feed on the back. "My pony was about to break down his stall door." She grinned sweetly.

Gus only arched one brow, then turned his back and lowered the tailgate of the truck.

"Need some help?"

"Nope."

Melanie shot Christina a dismayed look. Christina nodded her head toward the barns and mouthed, "Let's get out of here."

"Uh, Mr. uh. Gus. Last night, did you hear or see anything weird? Before the fire I mean."

"Nope. Just that kid yellin' 'fire' loud enough to wake the dead. Leastwise it woke me."

"Right. Well, thank you." Melanie shoved her fingers in the pocket of her breeches and backed away. When she reached Christina, her cousin grabbed her by the elbow and hustled her from the shed.

"Whew. That guy gives me the creeps," Christina said when they were out of his sight.

"Yeah. Which means he definitely isn't the arsonist."

"Why do you say that?"

"You've watched dopey horror movies before. The guy with one eye and bad breath is never the killer. It's always the handsome charmer."

Christina giggled. "Then we better interrogate Dylan."

"Give me a break," Melanie groaned, and they started laughing again.

When they passed the hay shed, Melanie smelled the burnt wood and wet ashes. She wondered if the investigator who had been poking around that morning had discovered anything else. Maybe the arsonist had been dumb enough to drop an ID card. At least then she'd be cleared.

"I called my mom this morning and told her about the fire," Christina said. "She was all worried, and kept asking if they should come get us early."

Melanie stopped walking. "Have they heard from my dad?" she asked, trying not to sound too worried. Part of her hoped he wouldn't find out about the fire. The other part hoped he'd called to say he was coming.

"No. Sorry."

"Not your fault." She sighed glumly.

Christina nudged her. "Hey, don't get gloomy on me now. You've been doing great. And we can't get distracted. Remember? We've got to win the team trophy and solve a mystery."

"You're right. Which means I better get back and finish polishing my boots before the afternoon lesson." Melanie said good-bye to Christina. As she plodded up the hill, she couldn't help but think about her father. It was only Thursday. If he knew he was coming Saturday, she figured he would have let her know by now.

That means he's probably not coming. She'd better get used to the idea.

When Melanie passed the house, she spotted Sean sitting on the porch swing talking into a portable phone. He had a big smile on his face as he waved her over. By the time she reached him, he'd finished his conversation.

"What's up?" Melanie asked, and she sat down next to him. Sean was one of the two campers who hadn't deserted her.

"That was a reporter from the local paper. He called and asked me a bunch of questions. He's coming out later to take a picture of me next to the shed."

"Oooh. I'm sitting next to someone famous!" Melanie teased. She stuck out her arm. "Will you autograph my hand?"

"Sure." He wrote his name with his fingernail, then picked up the phone again. "Now I've got to call my parents and tell them what happened."

Melanie stood up. "I'm going in for a cold drink. Can I get you one?"

He nodded, his attention on punching in the numbers. Melanie went into the kitchen and opened the refrigerator. The bottom shelf was reserved for fruit drinks and healthy snacks. She eyed the grapes and cheese chunks, wishing they were chips and candy bars.

She grabbed two boxed drinks and shut the door. Slowly, she sauntered back to the porch, pausing by the screen door. She didn't want to interrupt Sean who was retelling last night's adventure in an animated voice.

"By the time the firemen arrived, Dad, the fire was pretty much under control."

Melanie chuckled. Okay, so Sean was exaggerating a little. But she was glad he was getting his few minutes of fame. He was the kind of guy who needed a lot of positive attention. Especially since he was discouraged about his team being in fourth place, which wasn't so hot.

"Right! I'm the one who alerted everybody," he continued. "If I hadn't heard the loud noise outside, I probably would have gone back to bed. I never would have investigated, and we might not have gotten the horses out in time."

Loud noise. Melanie frowned. Slowly, she pulled the straw off the drink box. As she unwrapped it and stuck it in the hole in top, she thought back to last night. Hadn't Sean told Mr. Braznowski that he'd looked out the bathroom window and spotted smoke coming from the shed?

Oh no! Melanie choked back her cry. Her fingers tightened around the drink box, and juice squirted from the straw.

She'd *been* in Sean's bathroom. She'd *looked* out the window. There was no way Sean could have seen the hay shed. The house was in the way.

So how could he have known the shed was on fire, unless he was the one who had set it?

14

"I THINK THAT'S THE FIRST TIME MY PARENTS EVER SAID THEY were proud of me," Sean said when Melanie came out on the porch. He was just hanging up the phone.

"G-g-great." Melanie handed him his drink and sat down next to him. "Now are you going to call the president of the United States?"

Leaning back against the swing, Sean laughed heartily. Melanie told herself he couldn't possibly be the one who had set the fire. He was too nice, too cute, too funny. And he loved horses.

Still, she had to ask him about the window. "Sean, last night you told the fire chief you saw smoke. Just now you told your dad you heard a loud noise."

"Oh, right." Sean's lopsided grin looked sheepish. "Last night I was so excited, I told the fire chief the wrong thing. I did hear a noise. When I looked out the window, I couldn't see anything wrong. Still, I remember when Flash got cast the week before last, so I thought I'd better investigate. It wasn't until I ran toward the barn that I saw the smoke."

"Oh." Relief flooded through Melanie. His explanation made perfect sense. "I just thought I'd ask."

"Later, I told Braznowski about hearing the noise first. I mean, you can't even see the shed from the bathroom." He laughed but it sounded hollow. "I didn't want the guy to think I was dreaming the whole thing up."

"It wasn't a dream, that's for sure." Melanie shuddered. "More like a nightmare."

"Right." Sean drained his drink in one gulp, handed the empty box to Melanie, and stood up. "I better get Jester groomed for this afternoon's lesson in case the reporter comes before then." He shook his head as if disgusted. "Adrianne's been as picky as Dana lately. I think she and Nathan must have had a fight. Otherwise how can you explain the four points she took off yesterday for nothing."

"I don't know."

He waved good-bye. Melanie sipped her drink as she watched him go. Sean's stride was jaunty, his shoulders squared, and he whistled a lively tune.

Hardly the behavior of a mad arsonist, Melanie told herself.

So far, Friday morning was perfect—sleeping in, cool weather, and a trail ride. Well, almost perfect, Melanie corrected herself as she checked Trib's girth. Her father hadn't called yet.

She tightened the girth a notch, then led Trib down to Sterling's stall. "Ready?" she asked Christina.

Her cousin was standing by Sterling's front leg, frowning. She ran her hand down the mare's right cannon bone. "I think so. She's got some windpuffs from standing in the stall all night. I'll be glad when we're back home and I can turn her out."

"I'll be glad, too. I miss Kevin and Pirate. And Trib's been dying for grass."

Christina looked up at her. "You know, that's the first time I've thought about going home," she said. "I guess it's because the end of camp's almost here."

"Only two more days left." Melanie propped her elbow on the top of the stall door. "And you know what's really weird? When I think about going home, I think about Whitebrook, too."

Christina bugged her eyes out. "That *is* weird," she exclaimed with exaggerated horror.

"Oh, stop." Melanie giggled.

"Okay, team three," Eliza said behind her. "Let's get mentally prepared for the trail ride."

Melanie turned around. Flash and Trib were nose to nose. Trib squealed and pinned his ears. Looking surprised, Flash backed up hastily.

"That's right, big guy, don't mess with my vicious pony," Melanie told the Thoroughbred.

"So why do we have to get prepared?" Christina

asked as she led Sterling from her stall. "This is supposed to be a relaxing ride in the woods."

Eliza looked at her as if Christina had just arrived
from Mars. "Because Dana, Adrianne, Jody, and
Nathan are going to be watching the entire ride. They'll
note how many times our horses try and snatch grass,
how many times they try and kick another horse, how
many times . . ."

"Whoa. Stop." Melanie held up her hand. "We get
the picture. This is a trail ride without the fun."

"Correct." Eliza nodded solemnly. Putting on her
helmet, she snapped the strap. "So get ready."

The three girls joined the riders who were gathered
on the cross-country course. It was a huge group, probably the first time all the campers, instructors, and their
horses had been together. Melanie spotted Anita,
Jennifer, and Poe, and Nathan was easy to pick out since
his horse, Gulliver, towered above the others.

When she reached the others, Melanie checked her
girth once more, then mounted, careful to keep Trib
from walking off with her. Her team had inched from
fourth to third place, and she didn't want to blow it.

Jennifer came riding over. "Let's stick together," she
said in a low voice. "That way we can keep an eye on
each other."

"Good idea," Christina said. "You and Eliza know
trail etiquette better than Melanie and me."

Melanie groaned. "You mean there's a Miss
Manners of trail riding?"

154

"Mount up everybody!" Nathan hollered from the front of the group.

Sean and Dylan hurried toward them leading their horses. Sean's face was flushed. Throwing the reins over Jester's head, he stuck his toe in the stirrup to mount. Jester took a step sideways.

"Whoa." Sean snatched the reins, hitting Jester in the mouth with the bit before swinging into the saddle. Melanie had never seen him so impatient.

She steered Trib alongside Jester. "You okay?"

"Yeah. That stupid reporter showed up this morning instead of yesterday so I had to hurry. Plus, he says the article won't be in the newspaper until Monday. We'll be gone by then, so my parents won't even get to see it."

"I bet Perky will mail a copy to you if you ask her."

"Melanie! Over here!" Jennifer was waving to her to join the team. At the front of the pack, the riders were already heading across the cross-country field.

"Talk to you later," Melanie said, trotting Trib over to Sterling.

"Sean looks a little mad," Christina commented as they rode side by side, Eliza and Jennifer in front of them.

"Just in a hurry."

"Oh? Their team slipped to fourth, behind us. I would have thought that would make him mad."

Melanie furrowed her brow. "Is Dylan mad?"

"No. He takes it all in stride."

"Why's the team doing so badly? They're all good riders."

Christina shook her head. "I'm not sure. You'll have to ask someone on the team."

Melanie glanced over at Sean. Dylan was talking to him, but Sean stared straight ahead, a sullen expression on his face as if he wasn't even listening. "I'm not going to ask Sean, that's for sure. He looks too grumpy."

"All trot!" Nathan hollered, and the command was passed down the line. As soon as Sterling broke into a trot, Trib did, too. They jogged through the woods and down the hill past the log and bank jump. At the stream, Nathan gave the order to walk.

"Think Sterling will go across?" Melanie asked Christina.

"She better," her cousin said sternly, making Melanie laugh. Christina hated to yell at her horse.

"I'll go first. It's kind of muddy where the other horses churned it up." Squeezing her legs against Trib's sides, Melanie urged him into the shallow water. Halfway across the stream, Melanie heard a commotion behind her. She hoped Sterling wasn't giving Christina a hard time.

Melanie twisted in the saddle. Sterling was right on Trib's tail. She was cautiously wading through the water, snorting at the ripples as if they were going to attack, but otherwise she was quiet. But behind Sterling, Melanie could see Jester still on the bank and Sean was yelling at him.

As soon as Trib climbed from the stream, Melanie turned him around. Sterling splashed from the water, passed Trib and trotted after Flash and Geronimo.

"What's wrong?" Melanie called to Sean.

"None of your business!" He'd pulled Jester's head almost around to his leg. Turning him in tight circles, he repeatedly kicked him with his heels at the same time.

Melanie sucked in her breath. "Sean! What are you doing?"

"He-wouldn't-go-right—in!" Sean panted. Reaching around with one hand, he whacked Jester on the rump. The horse's eyes were round with fear. The reins were so tight, his mouth hung open and his tongue stuck out to the side.

The whole scene frightened Melanie. "Sean! Stop!" she screamed.

Just then, Nathan charged across the stream on Gulliver. "Sean!" he thundered.

The bellow must have knocked some sense into Sean. Loosening the reins, he slumped onto Jester's neck. His shoulders heaved as he gasped for air. Exhausted, Jester stood with his legs splayed. He trembled from head to tail.

"Get off the horse," Nathan said in a low voice. His jaw was clenched, his back ramrod straight. Melanie had never seen him so angry.

Without a word, Sean dismounted.

"You will walk your horse home. Bathe him, then

walk him until his pulse and respiration rates are normal," Nathan instructed. "Do you understand?"

Sean nodded.

"Melanie, *you* catch up with your team." Turning Gulliver, Nathan cantered back to the others. Too stunned to move, Melanie continued to stare at Sean.

"Didn't you hear what Nathan said?" Sean snapped as he whipped the reins over Jester's head. Then he started up the hill, Jester plodding obediently after him.

Trib danced in place. Raising his head, he whinnied for the horses that had left him behind. But Melanie couldn't move. She couldn't stop watching Sean.

Everything had happened so fast, the horror of the scene was just now registering.

Melanie thought she knew Sean pretty well. Only right before her eyes, he had turned into a monster. Suddenly, she realized she didn't know him at all.

She did know that for some reason he was different from the upbeat jokester she'd met that first week of camp. She realized Sean was down because his team wasn't winning. But was there something more? Something he was hiding that would cause such an angry explosion?

An uneasy feeling grew in Melanie's stomach.

"Melanie! Hurry up!" At the top of the hill, Jennifer, Christina, and Eliza waited by the edge of the woods.

Trib pawed the ground, eager to join them. Melanie glanced one last time at Sean, wishing she knew what was going on in his head. Then leaning forward, she relaxed the reins.

Trib didn't need urging. Breaking into a canter, he raced up the hill toward their friends.

"Done!" Melanie announced. Tossing the sponge in the bucket, she sagged against the support post of A barn.

"Good, you can help me finish." Next to her, Christina sat on an overturned bucket, her saddle upside down in her lap. The two girls had been cleaning tack all afternoon.

"Do I have to?" Melanie whined pitifully.

Christina aimed a dripping sponge at her. "Yes," she said in her meanest voice.

"Al-l-l right." Melanie picked up Sterling's halter. She hadn't told Christina about Sean's blowup. But she didn't need to. By the time the group had returned from the trail ride everybody had heard bits and pieces.

When the riders came back to the barn, Sean was cleaning out stalls. He had greeted everybody cheerfully as if nothing had happened.

Melanie had been baffled by the complete change. If she closed her eyes, she could visualize the furious look on Sean's face when he whacked Jester. She knew he was a good actor. Maybe the happy-go-lucky Sean was a fake, and on the trail ride, she'd glimpsed the real Sean.

A horrible thought crept into her mind. *Was Sean so*

angry and down he'd do something as desperate as start a fire?

No, Melanie answered her own question. The idea was so crazy. She quickly pushed it from her mind.

When the cousins finished cleaning tack, they took showers and headed for dinner. For once, conversation around the table was subdued. Tomorrow was the first day of the competition. Ashleigh and Mike would arrive around nine, in time for the morning's dressage test. Melanie still hadn't heard from her father.

Still, she refused to let it get her down. Instead, she was thinking about how well she'd done these last two days. Tonight, Perky was announcing the team standings. She, Christina, Jennifer, and Eliza had been working so hard, they had to have moved up.

"Chocolate cake for dessert!" Poe announced, breaking into Melanie's thoughts.

"Oh, Mrs. Henderson, you shouldn't have," Rachel said sweetly.

"Yes, she should have," Sean chimed in. He'd been cracking jokes through the whole meal, until he'd gotten all the kids laughing.

Melanie couldn't even look at him.

"Did you know you have clean up duty?" Christina asked Melanie when they'd finished eating.

"Not again," Melanie grumbled as she scanned the table. It was heaped with empty platters, plates, glasses, and bowls. "I'll be in here forever. I'll miss Perky's announcements."

160

"Not if you hurry," Christina said as she jumped up. In a few seconds, the room was empty except for Melanie, Mrs. Henderson, and Bekka, who was staring miserably at the heap of dirty dishes.

"Let's get a move on," Mrs. Henderson said as she bustled from the table to the refrigerator, putting away containers of food.

"Yeah. Yeah," Melanie muttered. She picked up the empty cake pan and walked around the table filling the pan with spoons, forks, and knives. Behind her, the screen door squeaked open, then shut.

Melanie looked around to see who had come in. A tall, handsome man with longish, graying hair walked into the kitchen.

Melanie dropped the metal pan. Silverware scattered on the floor at her feet.

"Dad!" she screamed. Melanie ran across the kitchen and flung herself into his arms.

15

MELANIE STARED INTO HER FATHER'S BLUE EYES. "WHEN DID you get here? Why didn't you let me know? How long are you going to stay?"

He chuckled. Smile-lines radiated from the corners of his mouth. He had a deep, California tan and his hair was sun-streaked. Melanie thought he looked as hand-some as a movie star.

"I flew in this evening. I wanted to surprise you. I'm staying until Sunday. Now does that answer all your questions?"

"Yes. *No*. Where are you staying? Do Aunt Ashleigh and Uncle Mike know you're here?"

"Mel?" Bekka's voice interrupted her questions.

Melanie stepped away from her dad and turned around.

"I'll finish cleaning up," Bekka said.

"You will! Oh, thank you. Thank you. I owe you one." Melanie guided her father to the porch. "Would you like dinner? Some juice?"

"No to both of your questions," he replied as he sat on the swing. "I grabbed a bite to eat on the way here. Not an easy place to find, by the way. I'm glad I got here before dark."

Melanie sat next to him. She was so happy to see him, she couldn't stop asking stupid questions. "But it's beautiful, don't you think? Susan couldn't come?" She looked across the lawn to the drive, half-expecting to see her step out of the rental car.

"No. Susan didn't come. Since it's a short visit, I wanted you all to myself." Settling back in the swing, he stretched out his long legs. "So tell me about camp."

"Oh." Melanie flopped back next to him. "That would take all night."

"Good. I have all night. Unless you have a special program or something you have to attend."

"Nah. Perky's having a meeting, but Christina can fill me in on anything important."

"Would Perky be Miss Perkins?"

"Right. She's English and pretty cool for a grown-up." Melanie told him about the teams, the points, and how much she and Trib had learned.

"What about the fire? Ashleigh told me about it over the phone."

"That was bad news." Melanie launched into the story. "And now Sean's a hero," she said.

164

"Did they ever find out who started it?"

Melanie looked at her hands which were clenched in her lap. She was afraid her father might guess from the expression on her face that there was more to it, and she wanted to tell him first.

She cleared her throat. "Um. They thought it was me."

"You?" Her father sounded shocked.

Melanie nodded. Her lower lip began to tremble. She had no idea what her father was thinking. She'd pulled some wild stunts back in New York. Would he automatically assume she was guilty? She wanted so much to show him that she had changed. Show him that now she'd never do anything as stupid or destructive as setting a fire.

Putting one finger under her chin, her father tilted her face toward him. "So camp hasn't been *all* fun?" he asked, his expression concerned.

Melanie's shoulders sagged. "This last week's been kind of rough. No one's come right out and accused me, and Christina and my teammates stuck by me. Still, it's made things awkward."

"Wow. That's heavy stuff to be carrying around."

"It is, but I can handle it." She smiled brightly. "Now tell me about California."

He wagged his finger in her face. "Uhn-uh. Not until I make it clear that no matter what, I'm on your side."

"Thanks, Dad." Melanie breathed a sigh of relief.

The slam of the front door made her jump. Sean strode onto the porch. In the dim porchlight, Melanie could see a scowl on his face. Without looking right or left, he leaped down the steps and took off across the lawn toward the barn.

His expression was as furious as when he'd hit Jester. Melanie's heart started thumping. *What had happened to make him so angry?*

She jumped from the swing. "Excuse me, Dad. I've got to find out what happened to my friend, Sean. He looks really mad."

"Go ahead," he urged. "I'm happy to relax here for a minute."

Hurrying across the porch, Melanie went through the front door and into the common room. Christina was talking to Poe and Anita.

"Psst. I've got to talk to you." Taking her elbow, Melanie swung her cousin into a quiet corner. "What happened? Why did Sean storm out?"

"Perky announced the standings. His team is last." Her cousin lowered her voice. "She didn't say it had to do with Sean's blowup on the trail ride, but it was obvious he lost major points." Furrowing her brow, she thought a minute. "But you know, he came into the meeting mad. He had a phone call right before. I saw him in the office, talking."

"Oh no. Maybe his parents called him."

Christina looked puzzled. "What's wrong with that?"

"I'm not sure. But you know how much pressure they put on him," Melanie said. "Hey, my dad's on the porch. Go say hi."

"Your dad?" Christina exclaimed, but Melanie was already out the door. She had to find Sean before he did something stupid.

Or dangerous.

"Be back in a minute!" she hollered to her father as she ran across the porch and down the steps. She had no idea what Sean might do. Maybe nothing. Maybe she was overreacting. But she'd witnessed what he'd done to Jester, and his anger scared her.

The barns were quiet. Melanie slowed to a walk. Her heart thumped in her chest. *Where was he?*

Hurrying across the green, she checked the hay shed. Fortunately, it was still light enough for Melanie to see. She walked around the blackened boards. The charred door was propped open. She peered inside the shed, but the interior was dark and empty. She blew out her breath. Maybe he'd simply run off to be by himself.

Melanie walked across the green to B barn. She noticed that Jester's door wasn't latched. Sean was in his horse's stall.

As she walked down the aisle, Melanie tried to think what she should say. Should she bring up his team losing points? The blowup on the trail? The phone call? Or should she pretend she didn't even know that he was mad?

But when she peered into Jester's stall, she forgot her indecision.

Sean was bent over, Jester's front hoof cradled in his hand. He had a screwdriver in his other hand.

Melanie flung open the door. "Sean Laslow, if you're hurting that horse, stop this instant or I'll scream bloody murder!"

"Cool it," he growled. "I'm not hurting Jester."

As Melanie caught her breath, she saw what Sean was doing. He had the tip of the screwdriver wedged under the rim of Jester's horseshoe as if he was trying to pry it off.

Melanie grabbed his hand to stop him. "Are you crazy? Maybe you're not hurting him, but you're not going to be able to ride him in tomorrow's competition, either."

Jerking his hand away from her, Sean continued to pry.

"Oh, I get it," Melanie said. "That's the whole idea. You don't want to compete."

"Right. So now that you've figured it out, Miss Nosy, scram."

She didn't budge. "Why don't you want to compete? What did your parents say to you? That you'd never win tomorrow?"

He paused for a second. "How'd you know about my parents?"

"Christina said you had a phone call and I guessed the rest."

He grunted. "Lucky guess. But you're wrong about what they said." Straightening suddenly, he dropped Jester's foot. His cheeks were beet-red. His eyes glowed. "Do you want to know?" he asked, waving the screwdriver in her face.

"They said if I didn't do *great* tomorrow, if I didn't prove that my riding was going to get me somewhere, they were selling Jester."

"But why?"

"Because they think riding's a waste of time. Because you can't get a riding scholarship. Because horses and lessons are too expensive. They've got a dozen reasons."

"But you love riding, and you're good at it."

He snorted derisively. "Like they care what I want to do. Like they care about me at all. I've done everything I could to make them proud of me. Now *I* just don't care anymore."

"But you *must* care what your parents think," Melanie pointed out. "You care so much that you'd rather forfeit tomorrow than fail."

When he didn't reply, Melanie knew she was right. Turning, he stuck the screwdriver in his back pocket, pulled out a comb, and began brushing out Jester's mane. Melanie was relieved to see he wasn't still trying to pry off the shoe.

"What about your team?" Melanie asked. "If you forfeit, they'll lose points."

"Who cares about them?" Sean retorted.

"I think you do. I think you care so much, you pulled all those pranks this week," Melanie answered, not sure why she said it. Except suddenly it made sense. Out of all the campers, Sean was the only one totally obsessed with winning. "You wanted to make the other teams look bad."

"That's crazy. Besides, the bridles on our team were switched. We lost points that day for being late to lesson. Why would I penalize my own team?"

"Because it would look suspicious if yours was the only team that didn't have anything bad done to it."

"Accusing me is pretty low, Melanie, and I thought you were my friend. Though a friend never would have told everybody about my blowup on the trail. You realize that it was your fault I got points docked today."

"For your information, I didn't tell anyone."

"And I'm supposed to believe you? The person who set the shed on fire?"

Melanie put her hands on her hips. "So you think I'm guilty, too?" she demanded.

Dropping his hand from Jester's mane, Sean faced her, a chilly look in his eyes. "You're the only one nutty enough to start something as dangerous as a fire. I heard about the horse you killed in New York."

Melanie recoiled as if she'd been slapped. Stunned, she could only stare at him.

"It was just lucky I woke up in time to see it and call for help," Sean continued, a hint of bravado in his voice. "Then had the sense to rescue the horses and set up the bucket brigade. In fact, for the first time in my life, my parents think I'm a hero."

Melanie couldn't believe what she was hearing. Narrowing her eyes, she looked at Sean as if seeing him clearly for the first time. And what she saw was a kid desperate enough to do anything to get his parents' approval and attention.

Anything. Even set a fire.

"Is that why you planted *my* flip-flop, Sean?" she said coldly. "Because you figured everybody would believe a *horse killer* like me wouldn't think twice about starting a fire in a shed next to a barn?" Stepping up to him, she stuck her face in his. "After all, everybody already believed I was the one mean enough to pull all those pranks."

Sean shifted uncomfortably. "No. I didn't plant your flip-flop. It was already behind the shed." When he realized what he had said, his eyes widened with fear.

"You *did* start the fire. You almost killed our horses!" Now Melanie knew for sure. Exhausted by the confrontation, she slumped against the stall door.

"Wait, you've got it all wrong. I did start the fire, but I didn't want to hurt the horses." Sean's bravado disappeared, and his voice rose with panic. "I set fire to the feedbags. I was planning on sounding the alarm, then immediately putting out the fire so I could be the hero. But the fire spread too fast. When I got back, it was out of control. Melanie, you've got to believe me," he pleaded.

Melanie couldn't look at him. "No. I don't have to believe you. Miss Perkins does."

Tears sprang into Sean's eyes. "I've tried to tell her a hundred times. But everybody started congratulating me and telling me what a hero I was, and for the first

171

time in my life my parents were proud of me, at least for a second."

"And it was easier just to let me take the blame?"

"I told you. That was an accident."

"It was. It fell out of my pack after the picnic. You could have told people it was already there, Mr. Hero. You could have come to my rescue." Melanie couldn't keep the anger out of her voice. "Go ahead and pull Jester's shoe. Go ahead and take the easy way out. I won't tell anyone you set the fire. You and I will be the only ones who know the truth. But don't you *ever* talk to me again."

Furious, Melanie threw open the stall door and rushed outside. The sun had gone down, and the duskiness of evening momentarily confused her.

But she had to get away from Sean.

Halfway across the green, Melanie stopped and burst into tears. Ugly memories rushed into her head—the horrible accident in New York, Milky Way's death, and Aynslee blaming it all on her. Last spring, what had started as a harmless, fun thing to do—taking the horses out at night—had ended in tragedy.

Suddenly, Melanie realized that what Sean had done wasn't any worse than what she had done. At least he had a reason—his desperate need for his parents' attention—while that terrible night, Melanie had only wanted a good time.

Melanie looked back at the barn. Sean stood outside the door, hands hanging by his side. His expression was so defeated, so miserable, Melanie knew he had told her the truth about what happened. He wasn't some horrible arsonist. Just a kid who'd made a terrible mistake. A kid who had been her friend before his anger had changed him into someone ugly.

And it was easy to recognize his anger, recognize what kind of person he was, because she'd been a lot like him.

Wiping away her tears, Melanie turned and walked back to Sean.

16

"I'M SORRY, MISS PERKINS." SEAN HUNG HIS HEAD. HIS words were barely audible. His cap was in his hands and his shoulders sagged.

Behind Sean, Melanie stood beside her father who'd accompanied the two kids into the director's office. When Miss Perkins had heard Sean's confession, she'd immediately picked up the phone to call his parents to come get him. Melanie and her father had convinced her to let him stay to the end of camp. In halting words, Melanie had told the director about the accident in New York. She'd told her how the horrible mistake had changed her life. Her father had added his agreement.

Miss Perkins took a deep breath. "You may stay and compete tomorrow and Sunday, Sean, mainly because I don't think it's fair to penalize your team. Still, apologies aren't good enough for something this major. When your parents arrive, we will have this discussion again. I'm sure they will see the gravity of the situation. Plus, tomorrow at the morning meeting, I expect you to apologize to your fellow campers."

Sean jerked his chin up. "You mean stand in front of everybody and tell them what I did?"

Miss Perkins nodded firmly. "I'm sure the thespian in you will rise to the occasion. You may leave."

Shoulders still drooping, Sean turned to go. As he passed Melanie, he didn't look at her. Melanie started to go after him. Confessing hadn't been easy for Sean, and since she was the one who'd convinced him to tell Miss Perkins, he might never speak to her again.

"Miss Graham, before you leave, I would like to speak with you."

Melanie stopped in her tracks. A warning bell buzzed in her head. What had she done now?

Stepping forward, the director placed her hand on Melanie's shoulder. "I want to apologize. When Gus found your flip-flop, I must admit, the seed of suspicion was planted. Plus, I knew from Dana's complaints that you weren't the most tractable camper." She chuckled. "Dana likes her campers to snap to attention. She referred to you as 'the one who needed three weeks at reform school.'"

"Oh, really?" Arching one brow, Melanie's father gave Melanie a stern look.

"I didn't mean to give her such a hard time," Melanie said apologetically.

Miss Perkins waved her hand. "You kept her on her toes. I also want to thank you for convincing Sean to come to me. I don't know what you said, but it was most effective."

Melanie wasn't sure how she'd convinced him, either. Fortunately, he'd recognized that his guilt was eating him up. If he hadn't been ready to confess, Melanie never would have been able to talk him into it.

"Now let's forget this whole ugly matter." Abruptly, Miss Perkins dropped her hand and striding over to Mr. Graham, linked her arm with his. "Let's give your father a tour of the camp."

"Good idea," Melanie said, glad the ordeal was finally over.

"I can't believe Perky's still letting Sean compete today," Christina said the next morning as the two girls dressed in their black hunt-coats and breeches.

"At first she wasn't going to," Melanie explained. "But my dad helped convince her to let him stay. I told her about what happened to me in New York, and how the mistake I made changed my life. Besides," she paused to adjust her white choker in the mirror, "Sean's not getting off lightly."

"Let me help." Reaching up, Christina took the pin from Melanie and stuck it through the choker.

"Argh! You got me!" Melanie grabbed her neck.

Staggering back, she fell against the bunk bed as if mortally wounded.

Christina rolled her eyes. "I don't know how you can joke around after all that's happened this week."

"Hey, as far as I'm concerned, everything turned out great. My dad's here. I'm no longer considered the mad arsonist or the crazed prankster, and our team's going to win!"

"Don't count on our team winning. Jason's here."

"Jason. Oh no." Jason was Jennifer's boyfriend. Last time he'd visited, Jennifer had gotten so nervous, she'd almost blown the quadrille.

"Besides. We're still in third place. And that's a long way from first."

"Do you mind if we don't win?"

Christina smiled as she buttoned her hunt coat. "No. The important thing is how much Sterling and I learned these three weeks."

"I agree," Melanie said solemnly. "And I learned a lot more than just about riding. I learned not to let my moods ruin things for everybody."

"So you would've been okay today if your dad hadn't shown up?"

"No way!" Melanie sputtered. "I still need to prove to him what a good rider I've become and how much I've changed so he'll let me stay at Whitebrook."

"You *better* stay at Whitebrook," Christina warned. "Who else will help me with all the chores my mom dreams up?" Standing, she checked her coat in the mirror.

A stab of fear pricked Melanie. It was almost the end of summer. What if her dad decided to take her back to New York with him?

"Now, tell me more about Sean," Christina said.

"Right." Sitting on the edge of the bottom bunk, Melanie put on her boots. "Miss Perkins told me that his parents are making him sell Jester in order to pay for the shed."

"That's horrible! I'd run away before selling Sterling!"

"Me too—if I had a horse, that is," she added quickly. She stood up, feeling stiff and awkward in her formal dressage clothes. "Ready?"

"Ready." Linking arms, the two girls left the dorm. Eliza and Jennifer met them outside. Melanie thought they all looked elegant in their white breeches and high-cut dress boots.

Hands on hips, Eliza eyed them with a sniff of disapproval. "Yuck. Black and white. We look like penguins."

Melanie and Christina stopped and stared at her. "Well, there's not much we can do about it. This is what we're supposed to wear for a dressage test."

"Not today." Whipping her hand from behind her back, Eliza held up four neon pink chokers.

"Hot color! What are you doing with them?" Melanie asked.

"*We're* wearing them." She handed them each a choker. "We want everybody to know we're the 'hot' team."

Melanie laughed. "Only old Frieda's going to turn 'cold' when she sees them."

Jennifer shrugged. "That's her problem."

"You mean you don't care if she takes points off?" Christina asked. "It could mean the difference between our team winning or losing."

"That's okay with us," Eliza said.

Christina and Melanie looked at each other, both dumbfounded by their change in attitude.

"I decided I found something more important than points and trophies," Eliza went on. "Friends who helped me get my dream horse and who made our team—and the past three weeks—special."

"But what if you don't get asked to become a junior instructor next year?" Christina asked. "You had your heart set on it."

Eliza's head drooped and she tried to look sad, but a grin crept across her face.

Melanie screeched and gave the older girl a hug. "You made it!"

"Perky told me this morning."

"Congratulations!" Melanie and Christina chorused. Then Melanie groaned. "Oh no, that means if we come back to Saddlebrook next year *Eliza* might be the commandant of A barn."

"Hey, she could never be as bad as Dana," Jennifer said.

Crowding into their room, the four girls huddled in front of the one mirror, trying to put on their chokers at the same time.

"Much improved." Melanie inspected her teammates as they stood side by side, rings of bright pink around their necks. "We'll definitely stand out."

After wishing Eliza and Jennifer good luck, Christina and Melanie hurried to the big house where Christina's and Melanie's dads were waiting on the porch.

When Melanie saw her dad, a rush of happiness filled her. He was dressed in khaki shorts, a Hawaiian flower-print shirt, and sandals. Next to him, Mike wore jeans, a navy-blue polo shirt, and sneakers. They couldn't have looked more different.

"Where's Mom?" Christina asked her father.

"Down visiting Sterling and Trib," Mike answered. "She missed them almost as much as she missed both of you."

Melanie shot a nervous look at her dad. "I hope that means I'm invited to stay at Whitebrook a while longer."

"Of course. We never thought otherwise," Mike said.

When her dad didn't say anything, Melanie didn't press it. She had enough on her mind worrying about the upcoming test.

"We better get tacked up," Christina said. "It's time to show the campers at Saddlebrook what real winners look like."

"And that will be . . ." pausing dramatically, Melanie pointed to her choker, ". . . the team in hot pink!"

*   *   *

Trib soared over the last jump as if he had wings on his hooves. When Melanie pulled him to a trot, the crowd of campers and parents clustered around the show jumping arena were clapping and cheering. It was Sunday morning, and she was the last rider to jump. Before she'd gone in the arena, she'd been so nervous, she thought her heart would thump right out of her chest.

Now it felt like it would burst with pride. Dropping her reins, she gave Trib a big hug around the neck. Every fence had been perfect, and it wasn't just because Trib was wonderful. She'd quit trying to prove she was a hotshot rider. It had worked. She'd been the perfect partner for her horse.

Still grinning, Melanie straightened in the saddle. Outside the exit gate, Christina and Eliza were hopping up and down, waving their arms. Since they'd jumped earlier, both girls had changed into shorts and T-shirts. Melanie waved back, glad to see they were happy for her, too. Then she realized they weren't smiling.

The bell rang from the judge's booth. Startled, Melanie jumped in the saddle. The finish line! In all her excitement, she'd forgotten to ride between the two flags.

With a groan of dismay, Melanie steered Trib out the exit. "I am so sorry, guys."

"Mel! That would have been the winning round!" Christina exclaimed.

"We needed those points for a trophy!" Eliza chimed

in, her face falling. Then the two looked at each other and suddenly burst out laughing. Doubling over, they laughed until tears ran down their cheeks.

Melanie stared at them as if they were lunatics. "What is wrong with you guys?" she asked as she dismounted.

"We're going to get a trophy all right. The trophy for the most boo boos!" Christina said, choking out the words.

Melanie started giggling, too. Yesterday had been both great and a fiasco. Eliza and Flash had performed a beautiful dressage test—then forgotten to salute the judge. Sterling had jumped a clean cross-country round—then balked at the water. Jennifer had had a clean cross-country, too—only she'd gone off course.

"Maybe we wore pink because we stink," Melanie said, sending the two girls into a second round of guffaws.

Her dad came up, grinning proudly. He'd put on sunglasses and a baseball cap. "Wow! That was super!"

Eliza and Christina hurried off, still laughing. "Did I say something funny?" he asked.

"No. I mean, yes. It was a good ride, but I blew it. I forgot to go through the finish line." Melanie smiled sheepishly. "That means our team didn't do too well."

Her father shrugged. "Not all my business deals are winners, either."

"You don't mind?"

He furrowed his brow as if puzzled. "What? That you didn't win?"

183

"Right."

"Melanie, you don't know how proud I am of you," her father said, his voice choking with emotion. "I was so impressed how you handled that incident with your friend, Sean. You've really changed since you left New York."

"I hope not *too* much." Standing on her boot toes, Melanie gave him a kiss on the cheek. "Does that mean I can stay at Whitebrook for now?"

"If that's what you want, it's all right with me." Her father gave her a hug. "Obviously, Kentucky has been good for you—in many ways."

Happy and relieved, she hugged him back. "It has been, except you know how much I miss being with you."

"We'll have to fix that. How do more visits sound?"

"Great!" Melanie grinned. Everything had turned out perfectly. And her father was right. She had changed since she'd left New York, even since she'd been at camp. She'd discovered that anger and disappointment didn't solve anything.

"I have to cool off Trib and put him away," Melanie told her father. "It's time for lunch, lemonade, and the big awards. And I just know my team will get one," she joked.

"I'll meet you at the house," he said, fanning himself with a crumpled program. "Lemonade and a shady porch sound refreshing. See you there."

"See you." Melanie led Trib down the hill. It *was* hot,

she thought running her finger under her pink choker. Unpinning it, she took it off. She'd keep it forever to remind her of the summer.

As she neared the barn, it looked as if she was the last to put her horse away. Most of the campers had bathed and cooled their horses already, though the barn area still teemed with activity. After the awards, Camp Saddlebrook was officially over, and kids and parents were packing up.

Melanie was sad to see it coming to an end. She'd miss her new friends. She'd even miss the intense instruction. At the same time, she was happy to be going back to Whitebrook.

"Mel?" Sean fell into step beside her. His hands were shoved in the pockets of his jean shorts, and he'd pulled a baseball cap low over his eyes.

Melanie tensed. She hadn't talked to him since Friday night. They'd avoided each other, which was fine with Melanie. She wasn't sure what to say to him.

Fortunately, all the members of his team, including him, had decent performances in the three tests, so at least he had that to feel good about. Still, after all the bad stuff that had happened, she wasn't sure she wanted to talk to him.

"I want to say good-bye," Sean said, his gaze straight ahead as if he was afraid to look at her. "And to thank you."

"Thank me?" Melanie was surprised. "I figured

you'd hate me for convincing you to tell Perky. I heard your parents are selling Jester."

"That wasn't your fault. You didn't make me set the fire." His tone was angry as if he was mad at himself. "Anyway, it worked out for the best."

"It did?"

He nodded. "Anita's buying Jester. She's crazy about him. The minute her parents came yesterday she started bugging them, and they agreed."

"Good. She's outgrown Mushroom. They'll be perfect for each other. Whoa, Trib." Halting, she turned to face Sean. "But what about you? Will you be able to ride again?"

He shrugged. "I don't know. But it's okay for now. Maybe some time off will do me good. There's a teen theater group that I might join."

Melanie's mouth tilted in a smile. "That sounds great."

"But what I really wanted to thank you for was . . ." Clearing his throat nervously, he scuffed the ground with the toe of his sneaker, ". . . for being there when I needed someone. I'll never forget that, Melanie."

Melanie bit her lip, trying to keep from crying.

Cocking his head, he studied her from under the brim of his cap. "If I write to you will you write me back? Even though I wasn't such a hot friend?"

She nodded. "Sure."

"Then expect a letter." He smiled once, then, squaring his shoulders, marched off.

For a second, Melanie watched him go. Then Trib tugged on the reins and stamped an impatient hoof. "All right, Mr. Spunky. Let's go."

"Melanie!" someone yelled her name. Melanie looked toward the big house. Christina was standing on the steps, waving her arms, "Hurry up or you'll miss the awards!"

Melanie waved back, then slowly led Trib down the hill. *I don't need an award,* she thought, smiling to herself. She already felt like a winner.

ALICE LEONHARDT has been horse-crazy since she was five years old. Her first pony was a pinto named Ted. When she got older, she joined Pony Club and rode in shows and rallies. Now she just rides her Quarter Horse, April, for fun. The author of over thirty books for children, she still finds time to take care of two horses, two cats, two dogs, and two children, as well as teach at a community college.